RICAN WRITERS SERIES   FOUNDING EDITOR Chinua Achebe

ER ABRAHAMS
Mine Boy

INUA ACHEBE
Things Fall Apart
No Longer at Ease
Arrow of God
A Man of the People
Anthills of the Savannah
Girls at War *
Beware Soul Brother †

MAS AKARE
The Slums

M. ALUKO

Chief, the Honourable
Minister

CHI AMADI
The Concubine
The Great Ponds
The Slave
Estrangement

C. ANIEBO
The Journey Within

FI ANYIDOHO
A Harvest of Our Dreams †

KWEI ARMAH
The Beautiful Ones Are Not
Yet Born
Fragments
Why Are We So Blest?
The Healers
Two Thousand Seasons

IAKO ASARE
Rebel

FI AWOONOR
This Earth, My Brother

RIAMA BÂ
So Long a Letter

NGO BETI
Mission to Kala
King Lazarus
The Poor Christ of Bomba
Perpetua and the Habit of
Unhappiness
Remember Ruben

VE BIKO
I Write What I Like §

OT P'BITEK
Hare and Hornbill *
Song of Lawino & Song of
Ocol †

NIS BRUTUS
A Simple Lust †
Stubborn Hope †

CHENEY-COKER
The Graveyard Also Has
Teeth

SS CHRAIBI
Heirs to the Past

✱ Four colour trade ed
* Short Stories
† Poetry
‡ Plays
§ Biography/Politics

WILLIAM CONTON
12 The African

BERNARD B. DADIE
87 Climbié

MODIKWE DIKOBE
124 The Marabi Dance

MBELLA SONNE DIPOKO
57 Because of Women

AMU DJOLETO
41 The Strange Man
161 Money Galore

T. OBINKARAM ECHEWA
✱ The Crippled Dancer

CYPRIAN EKWENSI
2 Burning Grass
9 Lokotown *
84 Beautiful Feathers
185 Survive the Peace
✱ Jagua Nana

BUCHI EMECHETA
✱ The Joys of Motherhood

OLAUDAH EQUIANO
10 Equiano's Travels §

NURUDDIN FARAH
252 Sardines

NADINE GORDIMER
177 Some Monday for Sure *

BESSIE HEAD
✱ Maru
✱ A Question of Power
✱ When Rain Clouds Gather
182 The Collector of Treasures *
220 Serowe: Village of the Rain
Wind §

LUIS BERNARDO HONWANA
60 We Killed Mangy-Dog *

OBOTUNDE IJIMÈRE
18 The Imprisonment of
Obatala ‡

EDDIE IROH
189 Forty-Eight Guns for the
General

KENJO JUMBAM
231 The White Man of God

CHEIKH HAMIDOU KANE
119 Ambiguous Adventure

FARIDA KARODIA
✱ Coming Home and Other
Stories *

ASARE KONADU
40 A Woman in her Prime
55 Ordained by the Oracle

AHMADOU KOUROUMA
239 The Suns of Independence

MAZISI KUNENE
211 Emperor Shaka the Great †

ALEX LA GUMA
✱ A Walk in the Night *
110 In the Fog of the Seasons
End
✱ Time of the Butcherbird

DORIS LESSING
131 The Grass is Singing

HUGH LEWIN
251 Bandiet

HENRI LOPES
✱ Tribaliks

NELSON MANDELA
✱ No Easy Walk to Freedom §

JACK MAPANJE
236 Of Chameleons and Gods †

DAMBUDZO MARECHERA
207 The House of Hunger *
237 Black Sunlight

ALI A MAZRUI
97 The Trial of Christopher
Okigbo

TOM MBOYA
81 The Challenge of Nationhood
(Speeches) §

THOMAS MOFOLO
229 Chaka

DOMINIC MULAISHO
204 The Smoke that Thunders

JOHN MUNONYE
21 The Only Son
45 Obi
94 Oil Man of Obange
153 A Dancer of Fortune
195 Bridge to a Wedding

MEJA MWANGI
143 Kill Me Quick
176 Going Down River Road

JOHN NAGENDA
✱ The Seasons of Thomas Tebo

NGUGI WA THIONG O
- ✳ Weep Not, Child
- ✳ The River Between
- ✳ A Grain of Wheat
- 51 The Black Hermit‡
- 150 Secret Lives*
- ✳ Petals of Blood
- ✳ Devil on the Cross
- 240 Detained§
- ✳ Matigari

NGUGI & MICERE MUGO
- 191 The Trial of Dedan Kimathi‡

NGUGI & NGUGI WA MIRII
- 246 I Will Marry When I Want‡

REBEKA NJAU
- 203 Ripples in the Pool

NKEM NWANKWO
- 67 Danda

FLORA NWAPA
- 26 Efuru
- 56 Idu

GABRIEL OKARA
- 68 The Voice

CHRISTOPHER OKIGBO
- 62 Labyrinths†

KOLE OMOTOSO
- 122 The Combat

SEMBENE OUSMANE
- ✳ God's Bits of Wood
- ✳ The Money-Order with White Genesis
- 175 Xala
- 250 The Last of the Empire
- ✳ Black Docker

YAMBO OUOLOGUEM
- 99 Bound to Violence

FERDINANDO OYONO
- 29 Houseboy
- 39 The Old Man and the Medal

PEPETELA
- 269 Mayombe

R. L. PETENI
- 178 Hill of Fools

LENRIE PETERS
- 22 The Second Round
- 238 Selected Poetry†

MOLEFE PHETO
- 258 And Night Fell§

SOL T. PLAATJE
- 201 Mhudi

ALIFA RIFAAT
- ✳ Distant View of a Minaret*

RICHARD RIVE
- ✳ Buckingham Palace: District Six

STANLAKE SAMKANGE
- 33 On Trial for my Country
- 169 The Mourned One
- 190 Year of the Uprising

KOBINA SEKYI
- 136 The Blinkards‡

FRANCIS SELORMEY
- 27 The Narrow Path

SIPHO SEPAMLA
- 268 A Ride on the Whirlwind

MONGANE SEROTE
- 263 To Every Birth Its Blood

WOLE SOYINKA
- 76 The Interpreters

OLIVER TAMBO
- ✳ Oliver Tambo Speaks

TIMOTHY WANGUSA
- ✳ Upon This Mountain

DANIACHEW WORKU
- 125 The Thirteenth Sun

ASIEDU YIRENKYI
- 216 Kivuli and Other Plays†

D. M. ZWELONKE
- 128 Robben Island

COLLECTIONS OF PROSE
- 23 The Origin of Life and De
- 48 Not Even God is Ripe Eno
- 61 The Way We Lived*
- 118 Amadu's Bundle
- 132 Two Centuries of African English
- 254 Stories from Central and Southern Africa
- 256 Unwinding Threads
- ✳ African Short Stories

ANTHOLOGIES OF POETRY
- 164 Black Poets in South Afric
- 171 Poems of Black Africa
- 192 Anthology of Swahili Poe
- 230 Poets to the People
- 257 Summer Fires: New Poetry from Africa
- 308 A New Book of African Ve

COLLECTIONS OF PLAYS
- 34 Ten One-Act Plays
- 179 African Plays for Playing 2

AFRICAN WRITERS SERIES
150

Secret Lives

Secret Lives

and other stories

Ngugi wa Thiong'o

HEINEMANN

Heinemann International Literature & Textbooks
a division of Heinemann Educational Books Ltd
Halley Court, Jordan Hill, Oxford OX2 8EJ

Heinemann Educational Books Inc
361 Hanover Street, Portsmouth, New Hampshire, 03801, USA

Heinemann Educational Books (Nigeria) Ltd
PMB 5205, Ibadan
Heinemann Kenya Ltd
PO Box 45314, Nairobi, Kenya
Heinemann Educational Boleswa
PO Box 10103, Village Post Office, Gaborone, Botswana
Heinemann Publishers (Caribbean) Ltd
175 Mountain View Avenue, Kingston 6, Jamaica

LONDON   EDINBURGH   MELBOURNE   SYDNEY
AUCKLAND   SINGAPORE   TOKYO   MADRID   PARIS
HARARE   ATHENS   BOLOGNA

ISBN 0–435–90150–8

Printed and bound in Great Britain by
Cox & Wyman Ltd, Reading, Berkshire

90 91 92 93 94 95 10 9 8

CONTENTS

Preface   xi

Acknowledgements   xiii

PART I: OF MOTHERS AND CHILDREN   1

Mugumo   2
And the Rain Came Down!   9
Gone with the Drought   15

PART II: FIGHTERS AND MARTYRS   21

The Village Priest   22
The Black Bird   29
The Martyr   39
The Return   49
A Meeting in the Dark   55
Goodbye Africa   71

PART III: SECRET LIVES   81

Minutes of Glory   82
Wedding at the Cross   97
A Mercedes Funeral   113
The Mubenzi Tribesman   138

For Nyambura and Wanjiku

PREFACE

Sometime in 1960 I met Mr Jonathan Kariara outside the Main Hall of Makerere University College and on an impulse stopped him: I had written a short story and would he care to look at it? Mr Kariara was then in his final year as a student of English: he was very involved in *Penpoint*, a journal then at the centre of the creative efforts on Makerere Hill. I had told him a lie. I was then in my second preliminary year, and the story was only in my mind. But with my impulsive lie, I knew I had to write a story. This later became *The Fig Tree* (*Mugumo* in this collection) and Mr Kariara was very excited about it: had I been reading D. H. Lawrence, he asked, and I was impressed and very encouraged. That was the beginning of a fairly creative three year period during which I wrote *The Return*, *The Drought*, *The Village Priest*, *The Martyr*, *Meeting in the Dark*, *And the Rain Came Down* and the first sketches of *The Black Bird*, *Mubenzi Tribesman*, alongside two novels and a play. In 1964 the well for short stories dried up. I attempted to write about my encounter with England and failed. Yorkshire Moors, Brontës' Countryside, the Scottish highlands, especially Inverness of yellow gorse and silver birches: all these were beautiful yes, but they only made me vividly live the Limuru landscape with its sudden drop into the Rift Valley. Memories of beauty and terror. I wrote *A Grain of Wheat*.

In 1971 I returned to Kenya from a one year spell teaching African literature at Northwestern University in Evanston, Illinois. I looked at the tired and bewildered faces of the people: I went to places where people went to drown their memories of yesterday and their hopes and fears for tomorrow in drinking. I visited various bars in Limuru, drinking, singing and dancing and trying not to see or to remember. A friend told of an interesting episode. A barmaid had been arrested for stealing money from an aged trader, her one-night lover. The friend who told the story was condemning the rather petty and amateurish theft. But I was intrigued by the fact that the girl had returned to the same bar and for a whole day lived in an ostentatious display of wealth and well-being. That was the beginning of the three stories (*Minutes of Glory*, *Wedding at the Cross* and *Mercedes Funeral*) which were meant to be the first in a series of secret lives. I also started working on a novel: how could I not see and hear and remember?

So that in a sense the stories in this collection form my creative autobiography over the last twelve years and touch on ideas and moods affecting me over the same period. My writing is really an attempt to understand myself and my situation in society and in history. As I write I remember the nights of fighting in my father's house; my mother's struggle with the soil so that we might eat, have decent clothes and get some schooling; my elder brother, Wallace Mwangi, running to the cover and security of the forest under a hail of bullets from Colonial policemen; his messages from the forest urging me to continue with education at any cost; my cousin, Gichini wa Ngugi, just escaping the hangman's rope because he had been caught with live bullets; uncles and other villagers murdered because they had taken the oath; the beautiful courage of ordinary men and women in Kenya who stood up to the might of British imperialism and indiscriminate terrorism. I remember too some relatives and fellow villagers who carried the gun for the whiteman and often became his messengers of blood. I remember the fears, the betrayals, Rachael's tears, the moments of despair and love and kinship in struggle and I try to find the meaning of it all through my pen.

On this road I have been helped and encouraged by many: Kariara, Joe Mutiga, G. G. Kuruma, Karienye Yohana, Ime Ikiddeh, Peter Nazareth, Hugh Dinwiddy, Chinua Achebe, and several others from Limuru. Encouraging, and touching too, have been the many letters from numerous boys and girls all over Kenya and whom I have never met. Currently I am deriving much pleasure and faith and hope from the exciting work being done at the University of Nairobi on African Literature, both oral and written. Taban lo Liyong, Okot p'Bitek, Eddah Gachukia, Chris Wanjala, Bhadur Tejani and other staff: hardly a month passes without our celebrating a literary event. And of course there is *Busara*, and the students' Writers Workshop, and the drama society, and new exciting names on the Kenyan literary scene: Kibera, Kahiga, Charles Mangua, Mwangi Ruheni, Jared Angira, to mention a few.

And above all there's Nyambura, beautiful Nyambura: from her I have derived the strength to rise from constant moods of despair and self-doubt to celebrate a few minutes of glory. Hence the present offering of secret lives.

NGUGI WA THIONG'O

ACKNOWLEDGEMENTS

Many of these stories have been published in various magazines including *Penpoint*, *Kenya Weekly News*, *Transition*, *The New African*, *Zuka*, *Ghala*, *Joe*, and some Russian and German journals. Some have appeared in anthologies too numerous to mention. *And the Rain Came Down*, *Minutes of Glory*, *Wedding at the Cross*, *A Mercedes Funeral* and *The Black Bird* are appearing in book form for the first time. *The Mubenzi Tribesman* and *Goodbye Africa* are being published for the first time.

PART I

Of Mothers and Children

MUGUMO

Mukami stood at the door: slowly and sorrowfully she turned her head and looked at the hearth. A momentary hesitation. The smouldering fire and the small stool by the fire-side were calling her back. No. She had made up her mind. She must go. With a smooth, oiled upper-garment pulled tightly over her otherwise bare head, and then falling over her slim and youthful shoulders, she plunged into the lone and savage darkness.

All was quiet and a sort of magic pervaded the air. Yet she felt it threatening. She felt awed by the immensity of the darkness – unseeing, unfeeling – that enveloped her. Quickly she moved across the courtyard she knew so well, fearing to make the slightest sound. The courtyard, the four huts that belonged to her *airu*, the silhouette of her man's hut and even her own, seemed to have joined together in one eternal chorus of mute condemnation of her action.

'You are leaving your man. Come back!' they pleaded in their silence of pitying contempt. Defiantly she crossed the courtyard and took the path that led down to the left gate. Slowly, she opened the gate and then shut it. She stood a moment, and in that second Mukami realized that with the shutting of the gate, she had shut off a part of her existence. Tears were imminent as with a heavy heart she turned her back on her rightful place and began to move.

But where was she going? She did not know and she did not very much care. All she wanted was to escape and go. Go. Go anywhere – Masailand or Ukambani. She wanted to get away from the hearth, the courtyard, the huts and the people, away from everything that reminded her of Muhoroini Ridge and its inhabitants. She would go and never return to him, her hus—

No! not her husband, but the man who wanted to kill her, who would have crushed her soul. He could no longer be her husband, though he was the very same man she had so much admired. How she loathed him now.

Thoughts of him flooded her head. Her young married life: Muthoga, her husband, a self-made man with four wives but with a reputation for treating them harshly; her father's reluctance to trust her into his hands and her dogged refusal to listen to his remonstrances. For Muthoga had completely cast a spell on her. She wanted him, longed to join the retinue of his wives and children. Indeed, since her initiation she had secretly but resolutely admired this man – his gait, his dancing, and above all his bass voice and athletic figure. Everything around him suggested mystery and power. And the courting had been short and strange. She could still remember the throbbing of her heart, his broad smile and her hesitant acceptance of a string of oyster-shells as a marriage token. This was followed by beer-drinking and the customary bride-price.

But people could not believe it and many young warriors whose offers she had brushed aside looked at her with scorn and resentment. 'Ah! Such youth and beauty to be sacrificed to an old man.' Many a one believed and in whispers declared that she was bewitched. Indeed she was: her whole heart had gone to this man.

No less memorable and sensational to her was the day they had carried her to this man's hut, a new hut that had been put up specially for her. She was going to the shamba when, to her surprise, three men approached her, apparently from nowhere. Then she knew. They were coming for her. She ought to have known, to have prepared herself for this. Her wedding day had come. Unceremoniously they swept her off the ground, and for a moment she was really afraid, and was putting up a real struggle to free herself from the firm yet gentle hands of the three men who were carrying her shoulder-high. And the men! the men! They completely ignored her frenzied struggles. One of them

had the cheek to pinch her, 'just to keep her quiet', as he care-
lessly remarked to one of his companions. The pinch shocked her
in a strange manner, a very pleasantly strange manner. She
ceased struggling and for the first time she noticed she was
riding shoulder-high on top of the soft seed-filled millet fingers
which stroked her feet and sides as the men carried her. She felt
really happy, but suddenly realized that she must keen all the way
to her husband's home, must continue keening for a whole week.

The first season: all his love and attention lavished on her.
And, in her youth, she became a target of jealousy and resentment
from the other wives. A strong opposition soon grew. Oh,
women. Why could they not allow her to enjoy what they had
enjoyed for years – his love? She could still recall how one of
them, the eldest, had been beaten for refusing to let Mukami take
fire from her hut. This ended the battle of words and deeds. It
was now a mute struggle. Mukami hardened towards them. She
did not mind their insolence and aloofness in which they had
managed to enlist the sympathy of the whole village. But why
should she mind? Had not the fulfilment of her dream, ambition,
life and all, been realized in this man?

Two seasons, three seasons, and the world she knew began to
change. She had no child.

A thata! A barren woman!
No child to seal the bond between him and her!
No child to dote on, hug and scold!
No child to perpetuate the gone spirits of
Her man's ancestors and her father's blood.

She was defeated. She knew it. The others knew it too.
They whispered and smiled. Oh, how their oblique smiles of
insolence and pride pierced her! But she had nothing to fear.
Let them be victorious. She had still got her man.

And then without warning the man began to change, and in
time completely shunned her company and hut, confining himself more to his thingira. She felt embittered and sought him. Her

heart bled for him yet found him not. Muthoga, the warrior, the farmer, the dancer, had recovered his old hard-heartedness which had been temporarily subdued by her, and he began to beat her. He had found her quarrelling with the eldest wife, and all his accumulated fury, resentment and frustration seemed to find an outlet as he beat her. The beating; the crowd that watched and never helped! But that was a preamble to such torture and misery that it almost resulted in her death that very morning. He had called on her early and without warning or explanation had beaten her so much that he left her for dead. She had not screamed – she had accepted her lot. And as she lay on the ground thinking it was now the end, it dawned on her that perhaps the others had been suffering as much because of her. Yes! she could see them being beaten and crying for mercy. But she resolutely refused to let such beating and misgivings subdue her will. She must conquer; and with that she had quickly made up her mind. This was no place for her. Neither could she return to her place of birth to face her dear old considerate father again. She could not bear the shame.

The cold night breeze brought her to her present condition. Tears, long suppressed, flowed down her cheeks as she hurried down the path that wound through the bush, down the valley, through the labyrinth of thorn and bush. The murmuring stream, the quiet trees that surrounded her, did these sympathize with her or did they join with the kraal in silent denouncement of her action?

She followed the stream, and then crossed it at its lowest point where there were two or three stones on which she could step. She was still too embittered, too grieved to notice her dangerous surroundings. For was this not the place where the dead were thrown? Where the spirits of the dead hovered through the air, intermingling with the trees, molesting strangers and intruders? She was angry with the world, her husband, but more with herself. Could she have been in the wrong all the time? Was this the price she must pay for her selfish grabbing of the man's soul? But she had also sacrificed her own youth and beauty for his sake. More tears and anguish.

Oh spirits of the dead, come for me!
Oh Murungu, god of Gikuyu and Mumbi,
Who dwells on high Kerinyaga, yet is everywhere,
Why don't you release me from misery?
Dear Mother Earth, why don't you open and swallow me up
Even as you had swallowed Gumba – the Gumba who
    disappeared under mikongoe roots?

She invoked the spirits of the living and the dead to come and carry her off, never to be seen again.

Suddenly, as if in answer to her invocations, she heard a distant, mournful sound, pathetic yet real. The wind began to blow wildly and the last star that had so strangely comforted her vanished. She was alone in the gloom of the forest! Something cold and lifeless touched her. She jumped and at last did what the beating could not make her do – she screamed. The whole forest echoed with her scream. Naked fear now gripped her; she shook all over. And she realized that she was not alone. Here and there she saw a thousand eyes that glowed intermittently along the stream, while she felt herself being pushed to and fro by many invisible hands. The sight and the sudden knowledge that she was in the land of ghosts, alone, and far from home, left her chilled. She could not feel, think or cry. It was fate – the will of Murungu. Lower and lower she sank onto the ground as the last traces of strength ebbed from her body. This was the end, the culmination of her dream and ambition. But it was so ironic. She did not really want to die. She only wanted a chance to start life anew – a life of giving and not only of receiving.

Her misery was not at an end, for as she lay on the ground, and even as the owl and the hyena cried in the distance, the wind blew harder, and the mournful sound grew louder and nearer; and it began to rain. The earth looked as if it would crack and open beneath her.

Then suddenly, through the lightning and thunder, she espied a tree in the distance – a huge tree it was, with the bush gently but reverently bowing all around the trunk. And she knew; she knew, that this was the tree – the sacred Mugumo – the altar of the all-seeing Murungu. 'Here at last is a place of sanctuary,' she thought.

She ran, defying the rain, the thunder and the ghosts. Her husband and the people of Muhoroini Ridge vanished into insignificance. The load that had weighed upon her heart seemed to be lifted as she ran through the thorny bush, knocking against the trees, falling and standing up. Her impotence was gone. Her worries were gone. Her one object was to reach the tree. It was a matter of life and death – a battle for life. There under the sacred Mugumo she would find sanctuary and peace. There Mukami would meet her God, Murungu, the God of her people. So she ran despite her physical weakness. And she could feel a burning inside her womb. Now she was near the place of sanctuary, the altar of the most High, the place of salvation. So towards the altar she ran, no, not running but flying; at least her soul must have been flying. For she felt as light as a feather. At last she reached the place, panting and breathless.

And the rain went on falling. But she did not hear. She had lain asleep under the protecting arms of God's tree. The spell was on her again.

Mukami woke up with a start. What! Nobody? Surely that had been Mumbi, who standing beside her husband Gikuyu had touched her – a gentle touch that went right through her body. No, she must have been dreaming. What a strange beautiful dream. And Mumbi had said, 'I am the mother of a nation.' She looked around. Darkness still. And there was the ancient tree, strong, unageing. How many secrets must you have held?

'I must go home. Go back to my husband and my people.' It was a new Mukami, humble yet full of hope who said this. Then she fell asleep again. The spell.

The sun was rising in the east and the rich yellowish streaks of light filtered through the forest to where Mukami was sitting, leaning against the tree. And as the straying streaks of light touched her skin, she felt a tickling sensation that went right through her body. Blood thawed in her veins and oh! She felt warm – so very warm, happy and light. Her soul danced and her womb answered. And then she knew – knew that she was pregnant, had been pregnant for some time.

As Mukami stood up ready to go, she stared with unseeing eyes into space, while tears of deep gratitude and humility trickled down her face. Her eyes looked beyond the forest, beyond the stream, as if they were seeing something, something hidden in the distant future. And she saw the people of Muhoroini, her *airu* and her man, strong, unageing, standing amongst them. That was her rightful place, there beside her husband amongst the other wives. They must unite and support ruriri, giving it new life. Was Mumbi watching?

Far in the distance, a cow lowed. Mukami stirred from her reverie.

'I must go.' She began to move. And the Mugumo tree still stood, mute, huge and mysterious.

AND THE RAIN CAME DOWN!

Nyokabi dropped the big load of firewood which she had been carrying on her frail back. The load fell on the hard floor outside the door of her hut with a groaning crash. She stood for a few seconds with arms loosely akimbo, and then sat on the load, letting out a deep, enigmatic sigh. It was good to be home again. It was good and sweet to rest after a hard day's work, having laboured like a donkey.

All her life she had worked, worked, and each day brought no relief. She had thought this the best way to bury her disappointments and sorrow, but without much success. Her life seemed meaningless and as she sat there looking vacantly into space, she felt really tired, in body and spirit.

She knew she was getting old. Only a few weeks back she had looked at her reflection in a mirror only to find that her formerly rich black mass of hair was now touched with two or three ashy threads. She had shuddered and consequently swore never to look in a mirror again. So old. And no child! That was the worry. It was unthinkable. She was *thata*.

She had vaguely known this a long time back. The knowledge, with what it meant to her and her social standing, had given her pain in the soul. A fat worm of despair and a sense of irredeemable loss wriggled in the very marrow of her bones and was slowly eating her away.

It was a kind of hopelessness and loss of faith in human life, that comes to a person whose strong dreams and great expectations, on which he has pinned his whole life, have failed to materialize.

Nyokabi's expectations had been many. But their unvarying centre had always been 'so many' children. Ever since her initiation, she had had the one desire, to marry and have children. She always saw herself as an elderly woman with her man, sitting by a crackling fire at night, while their children, with wonder-stricken eyes and wide-open mouths, sat around listening to her yarns about her people. She had got her man, the kind of husband she had wished for, but ... but ... Murungu had not sent her anything. *He* had not answered her cry, her desire, her hope. Her great expectations had come to nought.

A biting jealousy was born in her. She avoided the company of the other women of the Ridge and also the 'healing' touch of any child. Had the women, men and children not banded together against her? Were they not all winking at one another and pointing at her? All she wanted was to shut herself in her own world.

Even the old companion of her girlhood, Njeri, who had been married and lived on the same Ridge, had suddenly become an enemy. Nyokabi's jealousy forbade her to visit Njeri or call on her whenever she gave birth, as was the general custom. Nyokabi knew nothing about Njeri's children. So you see, her fatigue was not of an hour past, but the accumulated fatigue of a lifetime. Nyokabi remembered some little lines her mother had always been fond of chanting.

A woman without a child, a child,
Must needs feel weary, a-weary.
A woman without a child must lonely be,
So God forgive her!

She sighed and looked fixedly at her mud hut where she and her man had lived for so long. It occurred to her that her mother had been singing of her. Maybe she was cursed? Maybe she was unclean? But then her man had taken her to many doctors and none had offered a real cure.

Suddenly the pain that had filled up her heart, rose and surged up her soul, up her throat. It was all real, this Thing. It was choking her; it would kill her. The nameless Thing was too much for her. She rose and began to hurry away from her hut, away from the Ridge, going she knew not whither. She was like a creature 'possessed', driven on. The fire-eye of the sun, high up in the sky, was now on its way to its own place of rest. But the woman was hurrying away from home, unable to sit or rest. The Thing would not let her.

She went up the Ridge. She felt and saw nothing. The culti-vated strips of land sprawled before her, stretching down to the valley, merging with the bush and the forest. Women going home could be seen climbing up the slope carrying various loads. Njeri was amongst them. Mechanically, or as if by sheer instinct, Nyokabi avoided them. She cut across the fields and soon was in the valley. Through the bush she went, avoiding the beaten paths. The thorns tore her flesh but she pushed on, forcing her way through the labyrinth of the wild undergrowth and creeping plants. The wildness of the place, and the whole desolate atmos-phere seemed to have strangely harmonized with her state of madness. Even now, she did not know where she was going. Soon she found herself in a part of the forest where she had never been before. No light shone through and the heavens seemed to have changed. She could not see the smiling clouds any more, for the forest was very dense. For the first time, she hesitated, fearing to plunge deeper into the mysteries of the forest. But this nameless Thing urged her on, on.

A long rock stood in the forest. It looked inviting to a weary traveller. Nyokabi sat on it. She was beginning to come to her senses but she was still very confused and physically worn out. She could hardly tell the time or how long she had been walking. A voice spoke to her, not loudly, but in whispers –

'. . . Woman, if you stay here, you'll die – the haunted death of a lonely woman.'

She did not want to die. Not just yet. She stood up and dragged herself up. The heavy cloud of forlorn despair still weighed on her. But at last she managed to pull herself into the open. Open? No. The whole country looked dull. The sun seemed to have died prematurely and a dull greyness had blanketed the earth. A cold wind began to blow and carried rubbish whirling up in the air. The heavens wore a wrinkled face and little angry clouds were gathering. Then flash, flash, and a deafening crash! The heavens shook and the earth trembled beneath her feet. And without further warning the rain came down.

At first she was too amazed, too overpowered to move. A tickling sensation went right through her as the first few drops of rain touched her skin. Yes! The first delicate drops of rain had a soothing effect and she felt as if she could open her cold heart to the cold rain. She wanted to cry or shout 'Come! Come rain! Wash me, drench me to cold death!'

As if the rain had heard her dumb cry, it poured down with great vigour. Its delicate touch was gone. It was now beating her with a growing fury. This was frightening. She had to hurry home if she was not going to be drenched to death. She was now running frantically with all the vigour she could muster. She gasped with fear and all her life seemed to have become concentrated into one struggle – the struggle to extricate herself from the cold fury of the rain. But she could not keep up the struggle. The rain was too strong for a weary woman. So, when she approached the top, she decided to walk and abandon herself to the rain.

And then she heard the delicate but passionate cry of a human voice. Her womanly instinct told her it was a child's cry. She stopped and looked to the left. The rain had ebbed a little and so the cry could be heard clearly, coming from a small clustered bush just down the slope. The idea of going down again when her goal was so near was sheer agony for Nyokabi. This was a moment of trial; the moment rarely given to us to prove our worth as human beings. The moment is rare. It comes and if not taken goes by, leaving us forever regretful.

Virtually worn out, her goal under her very nose, the old

jealousy came and gnawed at her even more sharply. To save another's child! She began to climb up ... up ... But the rain came down again with renewed vigour, and a howl, at once passionate and frightened, rose above the fury of the rain. Nyokabi's heart almost stopped. She could not take another step. For the cry remained ringing in her heart. She turned round and began to go down the Ridge to the little bush, though she was tired and knew not whether she would be able to climb up again. The child, about two or three years old, lay huddled in a small shelter that had, until a few moments before, protected him from the rain.

Nyokabi did not ask anything but took the child in her arms. She tried to protect the child with her body as she began to climb up again, barely able to lift her legs. But, oh, the warmth! The sweet revitalizing warmth that flows from one stream of life into another! Nyokabi's blood thawed and danced in her veins. She gained renewed hope and faith as she went up, treading dangerously over the slippery ground. She cried, 'Let me save him. Give me time, oh Murungu, to save him. Then let me die!' The rain seemed not to heed her prayer or to pity her because of her additional weight. She had to fight it out alone. But her renewed faith in living gave her strength and she was nearing the top when she slipped off the ground and fell. She woke up, undaunted, ready for the struggle. What did it matter if the child was not hers? Had the child not given her warmth, a warmth that rekindled her cold heart? So she fought on, the child clinging to her for protection. Literally dragging her legs along, she reached the top. Then the rain stopped.

Wholly drenched, weary and hungry, Nyokabi trudged quietly across the Ridge towards her hut. Victory surged in her blood. A new light shone in her eyes, as if challenging the coming dusk. Her victory had overcome her very real phsyical exhaustion. She reached her hut, fell on the bed.

Her man was frantic with fright and worry. Nyokabi did not seem to see him. She only pointed at the child, and he wrapped him in dry clothes. He also brought some for his wife and added more wood to the bright fire, all the time wondering where Nyokabi had got the child.

Nyokabi had fallen into a sort of delirium and she was muttering '... Rain ... Rain ... came ... down ...' Then she would lose herself in some inaudible words.

After a time, he took a better look at the child. Nyokabi had by now fallen asleep and so could not see the look of surprise in her husband's face as he recognized the child as being no other than Njeri's youngest. At first he could not understand, and wondered how his 'jealous' wife could have come into contact with the child.

Then he remembered. He had met Njeri running frantically all over the Ridge looking for her child, who she said had eluded the other children. Great pride surged in Nyokabi's man as he went out with the sleeping child to break the news. To think his wife had done *this*!

GONE WITH THE DROUGHT

At long last, I also came to believe that she was mad. It was natural. For my mother said that she was mad. And everybody in the village seemed to be of the same opinion. Not that the old woman ever did anything really eccentric as mad people do. She never talked much. But sometimes she would fall a victim to uncontrollable paroxysms of laughter for no apparent reason. Perhaps they said so because she stared at people hard as if she was seeing something beyond them. She had sharp glittering eyes whose 'liveness' stood in deep contrast to her wrinkled, emaciated body. But there was something in that woman's eyes that somehow suggested mystery and knowledge, and right from the beginning shook my belief in her madness. What was the something and where was it? It may have been in her, or in the way she looked at people, or simply in the way she postured and carried herself. It may have been in any one of these, or in all of them at once.

I had occasion to mention this woman and my observations about her to my father. He just looked at me and then quietly said, 'Perhaps it is sorrow. This burning sun, this merciless drought ... running into our heads making us turn white and mad!'

I didn't then know why he said this. I still believe that he was not answering my question but rather was speaking his thoughts aloud. But he was right – I mean, right about 'whiteness'.

For the whole country appeared white – the whiteness of death.

From ridge up to ridge the neat little shambas stood bare. The once short and beautiful hedges – the product of land consolidation and the pride of farmers in our district, were dry

and powdered with dust. Even the old mugumo tree that stood
just below our village, and which was never dry, lost its leaves
and its greenness – the living greenness that had always scorned
short-lived droughts. Many people had forecast doom. Weather-
prophets and medicine men – for some still remain in our village
though with diminished power – were consulted by a few people
and all forecast doom.

Radio boomed. And 'the weather forecast for the next twenty-
four hours', formerly an item of news of interest only to would-
be travellers, became news of first importance to everyone. Yes.
Perhaps those people at K.B.S.[1] and the Met. Department were
watching, using their magic instruments for telling weather.
But men and women in our village watched the clouds with their
eyes and waited. Every day I saw my father's four wives and
other women in the village go to the shamba. They just sat and
talked, but actually they were waiting for the great hour when
God would bring rain. Little children who used to play in the
streets, the dusty streets of our new village, had stopped and all
waited, watching, hoping.

Many people went hungry. We were lucky in our home –
unlike most families – because one of my brothers worked in
Nairobi and another at Limuru.

That remark by my father set me thinking more seriously
about the old woman. At the end of the month, when my mother
bought some yams and njahi beans at the market, I stole some and
in the evening went about looking for the mud hut that belonged
to the woman. I found it. It was in the very heart of the village.
That was my first meeting with the woman. I have gone there
many times. Yet that evening still remains the most vivid of all.
I found her huddled in a dark corner while the dying embers of a
few pieces of wood in the fireplace flickered slightly, setting
grotesque shadows over the mud walls. I was frightened and
wanted to run away. I did not. I called her 'grandmother' –

[1] Kenya Broadcasting Service

though I don't think she was really so old as to warrant that – and gave her the yams. She looked at them and then at me. Her eyes brightened a little. Then she lowered her face and began wailing.

'I thought it was "him" come back to me,' she sobbingly said. And then: 'Oh, the drought has ruined me!'

I could not bear the sight and ran away quickly, wondering if my father had known it all. Perhaps she was mad.

A week later, she told me about 'him'. Words cannot recreate the sombre atmosphere in that darkish hut as she incoherently told me all about her life-long struggle with droughts.

As I have said, we had all, for months on end, sat and watched, waiting for the rain. The night before the day when the first few drops of rain fell was marked with an unusual solitude and weariness infecting everybody. There was no noise in the streets. The woman, watching by the side of her only son, heard nothing. She just sat on a three-legged Gikuyu stool and watched the dark face of the boy as he wriggled in agony on the narrow bed near the fireplace. When the dying fire occasionally flickered, it revealed a dark face now turned white. Ghostly shadows flitted across the walls as if mocking the lone watcher by the bedside. And the boy kept on asking.

'Do you think I'll die, Mother?' She did not know what to say or do. She could only hope and pray. And yet the pleading voice of the hungry boy kept on insisting, 'Mother, I don't want to die.' But the mother looked on helplessly. She felt as if her strength and will had left her. And again the accusing voice: 'Mother, give me something to eat.' Of course he did not know, could not know, that the woman had nothing, had finished her last ounce of flour. She had already decided not to trouble her neighbours again for they had sustained her for more than two months. Perhaps they had also drained their resources. Yet the boy kept on looking reproachfully at her as if he would accuse her of being without mercy.

What could a woman without her man do? She had lost him

during the Emergency, killed not by Mau Mau or the Colonial forces, but poisoned at a beer-drinking party. At least that is what people said, just because it had been such a sudden death. He was not there now to help her watch over the boy. To her this night in 1961 was so different from such another night in the '40s when two of her sons died one after the other because of drought and hunger. That was during the 'Famine of Cassava' as it was called because people ate flour made from cassava. Then her man had been with her to bear part of the grief. Now she was alone. It seemed so unfair to her. Was it a curse in the family? She thought so, for she herself would never have been born but for the lucky fact that her mother had been saved from such another famine by missionaries. That was just before the real advent of the whitemen. Ruraya Famine (the Famine of England) was the most serious famine to have ever faced the Gikuyu people. Her grandmother and grandfather had died and only she, from their family, had been saved. Yes. All the menace of droughts came to her as she watched the accusing, pleading face of the boy. Why was it only her? Why not other women? This her only child, got very late in life.

She left the hut and went to the headman of the village. Apparently he had nothing. And he seemed not to understand her. Or to understand that droughts could actually kill. He thought her son was suffering from his old illnesses which had always attacked him. Of course she had thought of this too. Her son had always been an ailing child. But she had never taken him to the hospital. Even now she would not. No, no, not even the hospital would take him from her. She preferred doing everything for him, straining herself for the invalid. And this time she knew it was hunger that was killing him. The headman told her that the D.O. these days rationed out food – part of the Famine Relief Scheme in the drought-stricken areas. Why had she not heard of this earlier? That night she slept, but not too well for the invalid kept on asking, 'Shall I be well?'

The queue at the D.O.'s place was long. She took her ration

and began trudging home with a heavy heart. She did not enter but sat outside, strength ebbing from her knees. And women and men with strange faces streamed from her hut without speaking to her. But there was no need. She knew that her son was gone and would not return.

The old woman never once looked at me as she told me all this. Now she looked up and continued, 'I am an old woman now. The sun has set on my only child; the drought has taken him. It is the will of God.' She looked down again and poked the dying fire.

I rose to go. She had told me the story brokenly yet in words that certainly belonged to no mad woman. And that night (it was Sunday or Saturday) I went home wondering why some people were born to suffer and endure so much misery.

I last talked to the old woman about two or three weeks ago. I cannot remember well as I have a bad memory. Now it has rained. In fact it has been raining for about a week, though just thin showers. Women are busy planting. Hope for all is mounting.

Real torrential rain began yesterday. It set in early. Such rain had not been witnessed for years. I went to the old woman's hut with a gift, this time not of yams and beans, but of sweet potatoes. I opened the door and found her huddled up in her usual corner. The fire was out. Only a flickering yellow flame of a lighted lantern lingered on. I spoke to her. She slightly raised her head. In the waning cold light, she looked white. She opened her eyes a little. Their usual unearthly brightness was intensified a thousand times. Only there was something else in them. Not sadness. But a hovering spot of joy, or exultation, as if she had found something long-lost, long-sought. She tried to smile, but there was something unearthly, something almost diabolical and ugly in it. She let out words, weakly, speaking not directly to me, but actually declaring aloud her satisfaction, or relief.

'I see them all now. All of them waiting for me at the gate. And I am going. . . .'

Then she bent down again. Almost at once the struggling lantern light went out, but not before I had seen in a corner all my gifts; the food had never been touched but had been stored there. I went out.

The rain had stopped. Along the streets, through the open doors, I could see lighted fires flickering, and hear people chattering and laughing.

At home we were all present. My father was there. My mother had already finished cooking. My brothers and sisters chattered on, about the rain and the drought that was now over. My father was quiet and thoughtful as usual. I also was quiet. I did not join in the talk, for my mind was still on the 'mad' woman and my untouched gifts of food. I was just wondering if she too had gone with the drought and hunger. Just then, one of my brothers mentioned the woman and made a jocular remark about her madness. I stood up and glared at him.

'Mad indeed!' I almost screamed. And everybody stared at me in startled fear. All of them, that is, except my father, who kept on looking at the same place.

PART II
Fighters and Martyrs

THE VILLAGE PRIEST

Joshua, the village priest, watched the gathering black clouds and muttered one word: 'Rain'. It was almost a whisper, spoken so quietly that a man a yard away would not have heard it. He was standing on a raised piece of ground looking thoughtfully at the clouds and the country around. Behind him stood a tin-roofed rectangular building from which thick black smoke was beginning to issue, showing that the woman of the house had already come from the shamba and was now preparing the evening meal. This was his house – the only one of its kind along the ridge, and beyond. The rest were mud-walled, grass-thatched round huts that were scattered all over the place. From these also, black smoke was beginning to curl upwards.

Joshua knew that in most of the huts the inmates had been sleeping with contracting, wrinkled stomachs, having eaten nothing or very little. He had seen such cases in the past months during his rounds of comforting the hungry and the suffering, promising them that God would in time bring rain. For the drought had been serious, and had lasted many months, so that crops in the fields had sickened, while some had dried up altogether. Cows and goats were so thin that they could hardly give enough milk.

If it rained now it would be a blessing for everyone and perhaps crops would revive and grow and all would be well. The dry anxious looks on the faces of mothers and fathers would disappear. Again he looked at the darkening clouds and slowly the old man retraced his steps to the house.

Soon it began to rain. Menacing thunderstorms boomed in the heavens and the white spots of lightning flashed across with a sharpness and fury that frightened him. Standing near a window, the priest, his horse-shoe-shaped bald head lined with short grey bristles of hair, watched the slanting raindrops striking the hard ground and wetting it. 'Jehovah! He has won!' the priest muttered breathlessly. He felt cheated, bitter and angry. For he knew that the coming of rain so soon after the morning sacrifice would be nothing but a victory for the rain-maker at whose request a black ram had been sacrificed. Yes. This was the culmination of their long fight, their long struggle and rivalry in Makuyu village.

Makuyu was an isolated little place. Even the nearest missionary station was some fifty-five miles away – quite a long way in a country without roads. It was in fact one of the last areas to be seriously affected by the coming of the white missionaries, farmers and administrators. And so while the rest of the country had already seen the rain-maker, the medicine-man and magic workers being challenged by Christianity, this place had remained pretty well under the power and guidance of the rain-maker.

The challenge and rivalry here began when the Rev. Livingstone of Thabaini Mission made a visit and initiated Joshua into this new mystery – the new religion. The whiteman's God was said to be all-powerful, all-seeing, the only one God, creator of everything. And the rainmaker had denounced his rivals when he saw how many people had been converted by Joshua into this new faith. He had felt angry and tried to persuade people not to follow Joshua. He threatened them with plague and death. But nothing had happened. The rain-maker had even threatened Joshua.

But Joshua had not minded. Why should he? Had he not received an assurance from Livingstone that this new God would be with him 'always, even unto the end of the earth?'

Then the drought had come. And all the time Joshua told the village that there would be rain. And all the time he prayed over and over again for it to come down. Nothing had happened. The rain-maker said the drought was the anger of the old God. He, the rain-maker, was the only person who could intercede for the people. Today under the old sacred tree – Mugumo – a black ram, without any blemish, was sacrificed. Now it had rained! All that morning Joshua had prayed, asking God not to send rain on that particular day. Please God, my God, do not bring rain today. Please God, my God, let me defeat the rain-maker and your name shall be glorified. But in spite of his entreaties it had rained.

He was puzzled; he could not understand it. And through the evening his forehead remained furrowed. He spoke to no one. He even went to bed and forgot to conduct the evening prayer with his family. In bed he thought and thought about the new God. If only Livingstone had stayed! All might have been well. He would have read from the black book and then prayed to his God and the rain-maker would not have won. A week later Livingstone would have prayed for rain at a public meeting. Then everyone would have believed and Joshua would have remained the undisputed spiritual authority in Makuyu.

A thought occurred to him; so staggering was it that for a time he could neither move nor breathe as he lay on his bed woven with rope and bamboo poles. He ought to have thought of this, ought to have known it. The new God belonged to the whiteman and could therefore listen to none but a man with a white skin. Everybody had his own God. The Masai had theirs. The Agikuyu had theirs. He trembled. He seemed to understand everything. Some gods were stronger than others. Even Livingstone probably knew this. Perhaps he feared the God of Agikuyu. That is why he had gone away and had not appeared all the time the drought had continued.

What shall I do? What shall I do? Then his way became clear. A sacrifice had been performed that day. Early in the morning, he would go to the sacred tree and there make peace with his people's god.

The morning was dark and chilly. The first cock had already

crowed. Joshua had just put on a big raincoat over his usual clothes. He trudged quietly across the courtyard.

The dark silhouette of the house and the barn beside it seemed watchful and ominous. He felt afraid. But his mind was set. Down the long path, to the distant forest, to the sacred tree, and there make peace with the god of his people. The birds were up and singing their usual morning songs, the prelude to dawn. To Joshua they had a doleful note and they seemed to be singing about him. The huge old tree stood where it had always been, even long before Joshua was born. The tree too looked at once mysterious and ominous. It was here that sacrifices to God were made under the direction of the elders and the medicineman. Joshua made his way through the surrounding dry bush and to the foot of the tree. But how did one make peace with God? He had no sacrificial ram. He had nothing.

'God of Agikuyu, God of my people...' He stopped. It sounded too unreal. False. He seemed to be speaking to himself. Joshua began again. 'God of ...' It was a small crackling laugh and the crack of a broken twig that interrupted him. He felt frightened and quickly turned his head. There, standing and looking at him maliciously, was the rain-maker. He laughed again, a menacing laugh but full of triumph.

'Hmm! So the whiteman's dog comes to the lion's den. Ha! Ha! So Joshua comes to make peace. Ha! Ha! Ha! I knew you would come to me Joshua ... You have brought division into this land in your service to the white strangers. Now you can only be cleansed by the power of your people. Joshua did not wait to hear more. He quickly moved away from the dumb tree, away from the rain-maker. It was not fear. He no longer feared the tree, nor the rain-maker. He no longer feared their power, for somehow it had all seemed to him false as he spoke to the tree. It was not even the feeling of defeat. It was something else, worse ... shame. It was a feeling of utter hollowness and hopelessness that can come only to a strong-willed man who has sacrificed his convictions. Shame made him move more quickly. Shame made him look neither to the left nor to the right as he made his way back, in the break of day.

The journey was long. The path was muddy. But he did not mind. He saw nothing, felt nothing. Only this thing, this hollow feeling of shame and hatred of self. For, had he not sacrificed his convictions, his faith, under the old tree? 'What would Livingstone say to me now?' he kept on murmuring to himself. Livingstone would rebuke him again. He would think him unworthy. He had once rebuked him when he had found Joshua quietly sipping a little beer just to quench his thirst. He had another time warned him when he found Joshua beating his wife because she had not promptly obeyed him.

'This is not the way a man of God acts,' Livingstone told him in a slow sorrowful tone. Yes. No one could understand Livingstone. At one time he would be unreasonably stern and imperious, and at another time he would be sorrowful. And as he looked at you with his blue sunken eyes, his head covered with a thick-rimmed sun helmet, you could never divine his attitude. Joshua was now sure that Livingstone would think him quite useless and unworthy to be a leader. He thought so of himself, too.

The sun had already appeared in the east when Joshua finally reached his home. He stood outside and surveyed the whole ridge and countryside. Suddenly he felt like running away, never to preach again. He was so deep in thought that he did not seem to see the anxious, excited countenance of his wife as she came out to announce that 'somebody', a visitor, had called and was waiting for him in the house.

Who could it be? These women. They would never tell anyone who a visitor was, but must always talk of somebody. He did not really feel like seeing anyone for he felt transparent through and through. Could it be the rain-maker? He shuddered to think of it. Could it be one of his flock? And what would he tell him after he himself had betrayed the trust?

He was not worthy to be a priest. 'If I saw Livingstone today I would ask him to give me up. Then I would go away from here.'

He entered and then stopped. For there sitting on a three-legged Gikuyu stool was none other than Livingstone himself. Livingstone, tired and worn out after a whole night's journey, looked up at Joshua. But Joshua was not seeing him. He was seeing something else.

He was seeing the altar on which he had sacrificed his convictions. He was seeing the rain-maker, listening to his menacing triumphant laughter.

Run away, Joshua! But he did not move.

Run away, Joshua! But he went nearer Livingstone as if for protection.

Do not tell him then! But he told him everything. And all the time Joshua had not dared to lift his head. He kept it down. And as he confessed, even this sense of utter hollowness and shame, he felt as if strength was ebbing from his legs. He was sinking down, down . . .; he leaned more firmly against the wall, with his eyes still bent to the ground. Livingstone had not spoken a word. There was complete silence. Joshua could hear his own heart beating, tom-tom, tom-tom. He was waiting for Livingstone to stand up and go, after upbraiding him and telling him how unworthy of his calling he had been.

Cautiously Joshua lifted his eyes. He met the full smiling face of Livingstone. Joshua was never more surprised in his life. The old sternness and apparent hardness of Livingstone was no longer in his eyes but only a softened, condescending sympathy of a man sure of a new and stronger follower. Joshua could not understand this look and his heart beat faster and more loudly.

With slow deliberation, Livingstone took Joshua's right hand in his and with the left patted him on the shoulder. He muttered something about a broken heart and contrite spirit. Joshua looked mutely at him. 'Let's pray,' Livingstone said at last.

Joshua's wife entered the room found them deep in prayer

and went back to the kitchen wondering what had happened.
When a few minutes later she came back she found Livingstone
talking about the problems of Makuyu now that the rain had
come and the drought was over. Joshua listened.

THE BLACK BIRD

Nobody really knew him. Even Wamaitha, who may claim to have been most close to his heart, never understood him. He lived alone. Who, then, could help him?

I remember him well. I remember him as a tall person with powerfully built limbs. He gave an observer the impression that he could have crushed anybody by the mere act of walking on him. His eyes were large and black and bright. There were some moments, though, when those piercing eyes looked imploring, or helpless, like a child's eyes. They made you feel for him. Or be afraid of him. Sometimes he looked at a wall and he would seem to be sucking in every detail. I don't know if he was subject to hallucinations but he would frequently start out of a reverie and stare around as if he had been woken up from a strange dream or nightmare.

I first met him at school. Manguo was then the only school in Limuru. And, so, many children came from all over the country to it. He came from Gathigi-ini Ridge which was several miles away from the school. He had to cross a number of hills, valleys and plains before he reached home. At school we called him Kuruma, meaning 'bite'. Funny, but now I cannot remember why we called him so. His real name was Mangara. He was a tall, athletic sort of chap. He was reckoned to be handsome. Girls liked him; but he shunned their company, as indeed he shunned the company of all. He was good at games and liked the tough kinds of sports like running, jumping and boxing. He especially loved wrestling and he would challenge anybody, even the older boys. If he was knocked down he would try again and though he was put down twenty times, he would never show any anger. At football, he had no equal and was the hero of nearly everybody.

At first I was not much attracted to him. Perhaps it was envy on my part. You see, I was not good at games and I could not shine in any field, not even in class. A chap who was popular, a favourite with girls and teachers, was bound to excite the envy of the less fortunate ones. I hated him. I hated his aloofness and what I thought was proud disdain of all favours or approaches for friendship.

And then I discovered his isolation.

I don't know what made me first notice it. Was it his eyes? Probably . . . It was, I think, at a school assembly that I chanced to look back and saw him gazing as if he was being very attentive to what was happening around him. But I caught him unawares. It was only for a second. When he saw me, he lowered his eyes and shifted his gaze.

Another time I came to school rather early. I strolled in the direction of the cemetery. Mangara was there before me, alone and deeply meditating. I did not speak to him.

My real encounter with him was yet to come.

Nobody went to the small dense wood below our school. The boys had got it into their heads that the wood was haunted. A woman, it was said, was long ago beaten by her husband so much that she ran away, and when she came to the bush, she died immediately.

What drove me there? I suppose I was feeling rather lonely. Anyway, it was during a lunch break when all the other boys had gone home that I found my way through the dense trees and bush and soon came to a large, clear, open place in the very heart of the small forest. There, sitting down all by himself, was Mangara. At first he was startled and annoyed at my intrusion. He glared at me. I stared back at him and so we remained, complete silence between us, till I broke it.

'What are you doing here?'

He did not answer at once. He looked at me and frowned a little as if he were weighing the question. I was irritated and was going to ask him again, when I saw him open his mouth.

'I am looking for the Black Bird.'

'Black Bird?'

'Yes,' he said, almost in a whisper, and still he looked past me. I turned my head to see what he was staring at. I saw nothing. I was puzzled. I thought his behaviour queer and immediately remembered that morning about a month earlier when I had gone to school and met him at the cemetery.

'I saw you at the graves.'

'Oh, did you!'

'Yes.'

'Black Bird again.'

I laughed. He laughed. Then he became serious again. I thought all this was a schoolboy's fancy.

'Have you found it?'

'No!'

I never gave it another thought. But a gradual friendship began to grow from our encounter.

We went through school together. He never mentioned the Black Bird again. He was a clever chap. Though he did not seem to put much effort in his work, when the final exams came, he had done very well and was one of the few boys who went to college. Our ways separated. I found a job with the T. & H. Trading Company at Limuru.

As a medical student he did very well. Everyone, including the lecturers, had great hopes for him.

'But what's wrong with him?' his fellow student once asked me as we were having tea at a café in Nairobi.

'Why?'

'He is always preoccupied with something. So strange . . . withdrawn, shall I say? And the way he looks at things . . . You might, er, think . . .'

It was while at college that he met Wamaitha, a girl teacher from Gicororo village. He became very much attached to her. I occasionally met him, and he would talk to me about her. He wanted to marry her. In those years his loneliness seemed to

desert him and he looked near what might be called happiness.
There was something hopelessly strange, almost tragic in his
childlike anticipation of happiness and union with this girl. I
met them together once or twice. She was tall and slim with shiny
black hair that was always neatly done. She was religious, at least
she seemed so to me, and even when she walked, she brimmed
with holiness. She was beautiful. Her beauty was not really of
the physical kind, but rather came from right inside her and
shone all over her.

One vacation preceding his final term at college, he unexpectedly turned up at our home. I stared at him with disbelief. The
haunted look was back in his eyes. He was now old and weary.
The brimful happiness had gone. I feared that Wamaitha had left
him. But I thought it wise not to allude to the subject.

There was a small room in our house which I loved, and we
used to sit there having our meal, or reading or chatting. One
evening, soon after we had eaten, we sat round the table, as was
our custom. The lantern was possessed of a devil and burnt
excitedly. Nothing passed between us. I was reading a book – I
cannot remember the title. I was not even concentrating.
Mangara was more withdrawn than ever.

'You have not heard of the Black Bird.' I almost jumped. I
remembered him as a boy in school. Our encounter in the
'haunted' wood came back to my mind.

'The Bird you were looking for at school?'

'Yes.'

'Come on! You are not serious.'

'I have never been more serious in my life.' He stopped. I
wanted to laugh but the tone in which he said this completely
forbade me. And then, sighing as if he had held his breath for a
long time, he said, 'Oh, I have been haunted all my life.' He then
looked at me and continued.

'You are not superstitious. I know you say you are not. Then
you'll think it strange that a medical student should be. But I tell
you it is not superstition. It is – do you ever think of the past?'

'H'mmm. Not very much.'

'You do not, for instance, think that the past can run after you and hunt you to death, in vengeance?'

'How?' I was puzzled. And afraid.

'Let me put it this way. Do you believe that something that happened long ago to your grandfather or father could affect you?'

'In what sense?'

'Ah, in every sense . . . Your father was cursed. Can that curse pass on to you?'

'The sins of fathers being visited upon the children unto the third and fourth generation . . . eh?'

'That is it, precisely.'

'Why, no! It is preposterous!'

He sighed. Then, talking to himself, he said, 'Oh, I do not blame you. But now I know that Wamaitha won't understand.' I was startled. It was the most pathetic tone I had ever heard from anybody.

'It was a Sunday evening,' he began abruptly. 'I was on my way home from a distant relative whom we called "Grand-mother". I was then young. The moonlight lured me to wander aimlessly over the Ridge and so it was late in the evening when I finally reached home. My mother was there. My two brothers were playing on a bed that was near the fireplace. They all looked happy. Father was not present. That was rather unusual as my father was not in the habit of being out late. Even when he went to the religious gatherings where he sometimes conducted prayers, he usually came home early. So, after a time, we all began to be anxious.

'I had just finished my food when there was a thunderous bang on the door. In a moment a ghostly dark form stood at the door. This dark form was my father. His usually neat and well-kept hair was dishevelled. His eyes were bloodshot. He stood there at the door for a moment without speaking, as if surveying the scene before him. Then he collapsed in a heap on the dusty floor.

'We all screamed in terror because we thought he was dead.

'Actually he was not dead. When mother sprinkled cold water on his head, we saw him slowly open his eyes. He seemed surprised to see us all around him. The terror took possession of his being so that he trembled a lot. He whispered something and the only words I could catch were "the Black Bird"! Nothing more. He slept again and did not wake till the next day.

'That was the first time for me to hear of the Black Bird.

'My father did not long survive the shock and died a month or so later. There was a lot of talk about his sudden death, for my father had been a very successful man, well-known for his religious fervour and honesty.

'He was followed to the grave by my two brothers who died of pneumonia. And so I was left with Mother. We sold all we had and ran away from Kiambu. We came to live in Gathigi-ini. It was then that my mother told me the whole story as far as she knew it – I mean the story of the Black Bird.'

Mangara paused and drew a breath.

'You see, the whole thing goes back to Murang'a. That was our original home district. We owned a lot of land there. My grandfather was the first of the young converts to the Christian faith brought by the whiteman. The new converts were full of zeal; they came to believe that what was in their people was evil. Every custom was a sin. Every belief held by the people was called superstition, the work of the devil. Our God was called the Prince of Darkness. My grandfather and the others like him considered themselves soldiers specially chosen by the Christian God to rescue a lost tribe from eternal damnation. Nothing could harm them. Christ was on their side; and so they went through the hills, treading on the sacred places and throwing away the meat that had been sacrificed to Ngai under the Mugumo. Soldiers of Christ fighting with Satan!

'Now, there was an old Mundu Mugo who had won much respect from all the people in the land. He could cure many diseases and he fought with Arogi and other evil men. It was said

that he could even see into the future. His magic was very powerful and he used it for the good of all the people, especially in
times of drought and war. To this man my grandfather came.
With great zeal, he destroyed the old man's things and burnt them
all to ashes. After that he began to preach to him. The old man
had not at first believed what he saw. Then in a terrifying voice,
he told my grandfather that he would live to pay for this outrage.
The old man disappeared from the land.

'Years later he came back. As a Black Bird. My grandfather
died and was followed by his children and wife. Except my
father. And they all said before they died that they had been
visited by a Black Bird. My father fled from Murang'a and came
to Kiambu. As you know, the bird followed him.'

Again Mangara paused. Then in a tired voice that made me
look up, he said, 'My mother died soon after we came to
Gathini-ini. She too had seen the Black Bird. I thought hard;
why should my father and my mother have died for a sin they
never committed? Why? Why? I then vowed that I would for
ever be on the look-out for the Bird. I have prayed and yearned
to come to grips with it. But all in vain. You may not believe it,
but to me, even then, the Bird was real. All through school I
looked for it. Then I went to college.

'I met Wamaitha. I forgot about the Bird. And all this time I
have been thinking of how to get on in the world so that I
might marry her. And, fool that I was, I thought I was becoming
successful. For it was success, success that I was after now.
Perhaps I thought this would rest my soul . . . and the thought of
the Bird never crossed my mind, or if it did, I tried to fight it
away by diving with greater vigour into my studies.'

He paused. He put his two hands across his head and leaned
back against the chair. He stared across, past me. Then he said:

'I have now met the Black Bird.'

I stood up and looked fearfully round the room. The fluttering
shadows on the walls were the incarnation of evil. I sat down
again and felt ashamed.

'It was last week. You know I did not come here directly. On Sunday I went for a walk with Wamaitha. I had never been happier in my life. For the first time, I seemed to have escaped from my past. I was a new man in a new world inhabited by Wamaitha and myself. We joked and laughed. Dusk was coming. We sat on a hill and played like little children. Wamaitha left me for a while and I lay on my side looking at nowhere in particular.

'The Bird was staring at me. I cannot describe the effect this apparition had on me. I felt nothing. I could not even shout. I just looked on, a little surprised at myself. Here I was, face to face with the Bird that I had always prayed to meet, and yet I could do nothing. The Bird was black; a blackness like soot . . . perhaps intensified by the dusk . . . But its eyes were large and . . . and . . . looked like a man's eyes . . . they were red . . . eh . . . no, NO. It was gone, and I had not moved.'

Mangara was greatly shaken by the recollection. I also trembled in spite of myself. I rushed to the door and frantically shot in the bolt. Then I went to the window and closed it, pulling the curtains to shut out the ominous darkness. Then I came back.

'Did you tell Wamaitha?'

'No! I did not. I told her I was not well. She could see me trembling. She thought I had caught a cold . . . How can I drag her into it all? In any case, she won't believe my story. Even you . . .'

I hastened to protest. But in my heart, perhaps to fight away the weakness I had displayed, I thought it a shame that he, a medical student and a man brought up in the European religion and ideas, should believe in such nonsense.

'I know you don't. Had it been somebody else telling me this, I wouldn't believe him either . . .'

Later in the night, as we were going to bed, he called me and said:

'You know, my grandfather should have gone for cleaning under the sacred tree. My mother said something of the sort before she died.'

That night I found it hard to sleep.

Mangara went back to college for his final term. I did not hear from him. I had now a better place in the Company and they sent me to Tanganyika to be in charge of their depot. I was flattered, for I was the first African to hold such a post in the Company.

I was in Tanganyika for six months before I returned home for a short visit. Limuru had not changed much. A new site for building a trading centre had been measured out but the old Indian Bazaar was still there. I went through the Bazaar and came to the small path that would take me home. It was there that I met Wamaitha. She had changed. She was thin and tall and her face wore a haggard look. The dress she wore had not been washed for a week. Strange. Where was her bright, holy look? Where was Mangara?

'How is it with you?' I said as I shook her thin hand.

'I'm well.'

'How is Mangara?' I cheerfully asked.

She stared at me. I stared back. My question seemed to have hurt her.

'Haven't you heard?'

'Heard what?'

'He's dead.'

'Dead!'

'He failed his exam. So, people say, he committed suicide ... Oh! Oh! Why could he not trust me? I would have loved him all the same ...'

She cried freely, as if the death was still fresh in her mind. I did not know what to think. How could he have failed the exam?

A week later I went to see Dr K., also a graduate of that college, because I had a pain in my chest and was coughing a lot. The change of climate, I suppose. We talked a lot. The talk drifted to Mangara's death.

'People say he committed suicide because he failed. I don't

believe it. That man was strange. He was bright, though. None of us could measure against him. But in the last term he neglected all study. He grew thinner day by day. In the evening he would be seen round the college chapel. He seemed to have no life. But during the exam his eyes were strangely bright as if he was seeing something beautiful and exciting . . . When the results came, he had failed. He learnt about the results here. I was with him. I tell you he was not in the least shocked. It was as if he had known this all along. A week later he was found dead under the sacred tree. His eyes wore a strange look of peace, you know, as if he had accomplished a difficult task. The look you sometimes see in the revivalists.'

When I got home I went to bed straight away. But for a long time I only stared into space, unable to decide whether to put out the light or not.

THE MARTYR

When Mr and Mrs Garstone were murdered in their home by unknown gangsters, there was a lot of talk about it. It was all on the front pages of the daily papers and figured importantly in the Radio Newsreel. Perhaps this was so because they were the first European settlers to be killed in the increased wave of violence that had spread all over the country. The violence was said to have political motives. And wherever you went, in the market-places, in the Indian bazaars, in a remote African duka, you were bound to hear something about the murder. There were a variety of accounts and interpretations.

Nowhere was the matter more thoroughly discussed than in a remote, lonely house built on a hill, which belonged, quite appropriately, to Mrs Hill. Her husband, an old veteran settler of the pioneering period, had died the previous year after an attack of malaria while on a visit to Uganda. Her only son and daughter were now getting their education at 'Home' – home being another name for England. Being one of the earliest settlers and owning a lot of land with big tea plantations sprawling right across the country, she was much respected by the others if not liked by all.

For some did not like what they considered her too 'liberal' attitude to the 'natives'. When Mrs Smiles and Mrs Hardy came into her house two days later to discuss the murder, they wore a look of sad triumph – sad because Europeans (not just Mr and Mrs Garstone) had been killed, and of triumph, because the essential depravity and ingratitude of the natives had been demonstrated beyond all doubt. No longer could Mrs Hill maintain that natives could be civilized if only they were handled in the right manner.

Mrs Smiles was a lean, middle-aged woman whose tough,

determined nose and tight lips reminded one so vividly of a missionary. In a sense she was. Convinced that she and her kind formed an oasis of civilization in a wild country of savage people, she considered it almost her calling to keep on reminding the natives and anyone else of the fact, by her gait, talk and general bearing.

Mrs Hardy was of Boer descent and had early migrated into the country from South Africa. Having no opinions of her own about anything, she mostly found herself agreeing with any views that most approximated those of her husband and her race. For instance, on this day she found herself in agreement with whatever Mrs Smiles said. Mrs Hill stuck to her guns and maintained, as indeed she had always done, that the natives were obedient at heart and *all* you needed was to treat them kindly.

'That's all they need. *Treat them kindly*. They will take kindly to you. Look at my "boys". They all love me. They would do anything I ask them to!' That was her philosophy and it was shared by quite a number of the liberal, progressive type. Mrs Hill had done some liberal things for her 'boys'. Not only had she built some brick quarters (*brick*, mind you) but had also put up a school for the children. It did not matter if the school had not enough teachers or if the children learnt only half a day and worked in the plantations for the other half; it was more than most other settlers had the courage to do!

'It is horrible. Oh, a horrible act,' declared Mrs Smiles rather vehemently. Mrs Hardy agreed. Mrs Hill remained neutral.

'How could they do it? We've brought 'em civilization. We've stopped slavery and tribal wars. Were they not all leading savage miserable lives?' Mrs Smiles spoke with all her powers of oratory. Then she concluded with a sad shake of the head: 'But I've always said they'll never be civilized, simply can't take it.'

'We should show tolerance,' suggested Mrs Hill. Her tone spoke more of the missionary than Mrs Smiles's looks.

'Tolerant! Tolerant! How long shall we continue being tolerant? Who could have been more tolerant than the Garstones? Who more kind? And to think of all the squatters they maintained!

'Well, it isn't the squatters who ...'

'Who did? Who did?'

'They should all be hanged!' suggested Mrs Hardy. There was conviction in her voice.

'And to think they were actually called from bed by their houseboy!'

'Indeed?'

'Yes. It was their houseboy who knocked at their door and urgently asked them to open. Said some people were after him –'

'Perhaps there –'

'No! It was all planned. All a trick. As soon as the door was opened, the gang rushed in. It's all in the paper.'

Mrs Hill looked away rather guiltily. She had not read her paper.

It was time for tea. She excused herself and went near the door and called out in a kind, shrill voice.

'Njoroge! Njoroge!'

Njoroge was her 'houseboy'. He was a tall, broad-shouldered man nearing middle age. He had been in the Hills' service for more than ten years. He wore green trousers, with a red cloth-band round the waist and a red fez on his head. He now appeared at the door and raised his eyebrows in inquiry – an action which with him accompanied the words, 'Yes, Memsahib?' or 'Ndio, Bwana.'

'Leta Chai.'

'Ndio, Memsahib!' and he vanished back after casting a quick glance round all the Memsahibs there assembled. The conversation which had been interrupted by Njoroge's appearance was now resumed.

'They look so innocent,' said Mrs Hardy.

'Yes. Quite the innocent flower but the serpent under it.' Mrs Smiles was acquainted with Shakespeare.

'Been with me for ten years or so. Very faithful. Likes me very much.' Mrs Hill was defending her 'boy'.

'All the same I don't like him. I don't like his face.'

'The same with me.'

Tea was brought. They drank, still chatting about the death, the government's policy, and the political demagogues who were undesirable elements in this otherwise beautiful country. But Mrs Hill, maintained that these semi-illiterate demagogues who went to Britain and thought they had education did not know the true aspirations of their people. You could still win your 'boys' by being kind to them.

Nevertheless, when Mrs Smiles and Mrs Hardy had gone, she brooded over that murder and the conversation. She felt uneasy and for the first time noticed that she lived a bit too far from any help in case of an attack. The knowledge that she had a pistol was a comfort.

Supper was over. That ended Njoroge's day. He stepped out of the light into the countless shadows and then vanished into the darkness. He was following the footpath from Mrs Hill's house to the workers' quarters down the hill. He tried to whistle to dispel the silence and loneliness that hung around him. He could not. Instead he heard a bird cry, sharp, shrill. Strange thing for a bird to cry at night.

He stopped, stood stock-still. Below, he could perceive nothing. But behind him the immense silhouette of Memsahib's house – large, imposing – could be seen. He looked back intently, angrily. In his anger, he suddenly thought he was growing old.

'You. You. I've lived with you so long. And you've reduced me to this!' Njoroge wanted to shout to the house all this and many other things that had long accumulated in his heart. The house would not respond. He felt foolish and moved on.

Again the bird cried. Twice!

'A warning to her,' Njoroge thought. And again his whole soul rose in anger – anger against those with a white skin, those

foreign elements that had displaced the true sons of the land
from their God-given place. Had God not promised Gekoyo all
this land, he and his children, forever and ever? Now the land
had been taken away.

He remembered his father, as he always did when these
moments of anger and bitterness possessed him. He had died in
the struggle – the struggle to rebuild the destroyed shrines.
That was at the famous 1923 Nairobi Massacre when police fired
on a people peacefully demonstrating for their rights. His father
was among the people who died. Since then Njoroge had had to
struggle for a living – seeking employment here and there on
European farms. He had met many types – some harsh, some
kind, but all dominating, giving him just what salary they
thought fit for him. Then he had come to be employed by the
Hills. It was a strange coincidence that he had come here. A big
portion of the land now occupied by Mrs Hill was the land his
father had shown him as belonging to the family. They had found
the land occupied when his father and some of the others had
temporarily retired to Muranga owing to famine. They had come
back and *Ng'o!* the land was gone.

'Do you see that fig tree? Remember that land is yours. Be
patient. Watch these Europeans. They will go and then you
can claim the land.'

He was small then. After his father's death, Njoroge had
forgotten this injunction. But when he coincidentally came here
and saw the tree, he remembered. He knew it all – all by heart.
He knew where every boundary went through.

Njoroge had never liked Mrs Hill. He had always resented her
complacency in thinking she had done so much for the workers.
He had worked with cruel types like Mrs Smiles and Mrs Hardy.
But he always knew where he stood with such. But Mrs Hill!
Her liberalism was almost smothering. Njoroge hated settlers.
He hated above all what he thought was their hypocrisy and
complacency. He knew that Mrs Hill was no exception. She was
like all the others, only she loved paternalism. It convinced her

she was better than the others. But she was worse. You did not know exactly where you stood with her.

All of a sudden, Njoroge shouted, 'I hate them! I hate them!' Then a grim satisfaction came over him. Tonight, anyway, Mrs Hill would die – pay for her own smug liberalism, her paternalism and pay for all the sins of her settler race. It would be one settler less.

He came to his own room. There was no smoke coming from all the other rooms belonging to the other workers. The lights had even gone out in many of them. Perhaps, some were already asleep or gone to the Native Reserve to drink beer. He lit the lantern and sat on the bed. It was a very small room. Sitting on the bed one could almost touch all the corners of the room if one stretched one's arms wide. Yet it was here, *here*, that he with two wives and a number of children had to live, had in fact lived for more than five years. So crammed! Yet Mrs Hill thought that she had done enough by just having the houses built with brick.

'Mzuri, sana, eh?' (very good, eh?) she was very fond of asking. And whenever she had visitors she brought them to the edge of the hill and pointed at the houses.

Again Njoroge smiled grimly to think how Mrs Hill would pay for all this self-congratulatory piety. He also knew that he had an axe to grind. He had to avenge the death of his father and strike a blow for the occupied family land. It was foresight on his part to have taken his wives and children back to the Reserve. They might else have been in the way and in any case he did not want to bring trouble to them should he be forced to run away after the act.

The other Ihii (Freedom Boys) would come at any time now. He would lead them to the house. Treacherous – yes! But how necessary.

The cry of the night bird, this time louder than ever, reached his ears. That was a bad omen. It always portended death – death for Mrs Hill. He thought of her. He remembered her. He had lived with Memsahib and Bwana for more than ten years. He knew that she had loved her husband. Of that he was sure. She almost died of grief when she had learnt of his death. In that moment her settlerism had been shorn off. In that naked moment, Njoroge had been able to pity her. Then the children! He had known them. He had seen them grow up like any other children. Almost like his own. They loved their parents, and Mrs Hill had always been so tender with them, so loving. He thought of them in England, wherever that was, fatherless and motherless.

And then he realized, too suddenly, that he could not do it. He could not tell how, but Mrs Hill had suddenly crystallized into a woman, a wife, somebody like Njeri or Wambui, and above all, a mother. He could not kill a woman. He could not kill a mother. He hated himself for this change. He felt agitated. He tried hard to put himself in the other condition, his former self and see her as just a settler. As a settler, it was easy. For Njoroge hated settlers and all Europeans. If only he could see her like this (as one among many white men or settlers) then he could do it. Without scruples. But he could not bring back the other self. Not now, anyway. He had never thought of her in these terms. Until today. And yet he knew she was the same, and would be the same tomorrow – a patronizing, complacent woman. It was then he knew that he was a divided man and perhaps would ever remain like that. For now it even seemed an impossible thing to snap just like that ten years of relationship, though to him they had been years of pain and shame. He prayed and wished there had never been injustices. Then there would never have been this rift – the rift between white and black. Then he would never have been put in this painful situation.

What was he to do now? Would he betray the 'Boys'? He sat there, irresolute, unable to decide on a course of action. If only he had not thought of her in human terms! That he hated settlers was quite clear in his mind. But to kill a mother of two seemed too painful a task for him to do in a free frame of mind.

He went out.

Darkness still covered him and he could see nothing clearly. The stars above seemed to be anxiously awaiting Njoroge's decision. Then, as if their cold stare was compelling him, he began to walk, walk back to Mrs Hill's house. He had decided to save her. Then probably he would go to the forest. There, he would forever fight with a freer conscience. That seemed excellent. It would also serve as a propitiation for his betrayal of the other 'Boys'.

There was no time to lose. It was already late and the 'Boys' might come any time. So he ran with one purpose – to save the woman. At the road he heard footsteps. He stepped into the bush and lay still. He was certain that those were the 'Boys'. He waited breathlessly for the footsteps to die. Again he hated himself for this betrayal. But how could he fail to hearken to this other voice? He ran on when the footsteps had died. It was necessary to run, for if the 'Boys' discovered his betrayal he would surely meet death. But then he did not mind this. He only wanted to finish this other task first.

At last, sweating and panting, he reached Mrs Hill's house and knocked at the door, crying, 'Memsahib! Memsahib!'

Mrs Hill had not yet gone to bed. She had sat up, a multitude of thoughts crossing her mind. Ever since that afternoon's conversation with the other women, she had felt more and more uneasy. When Njoroge went and she was left alone she had gone to her safe and taken out her pistol, with which she was now toying. It was better to be prepared. It was unfortunate that her husband had died. He might have kept her company.

She sighed over and over again as she remembered her pioneering days. She and her husband and others had tamed the wilderness of this country and had developed a whole mass of unoccupied land. People like Njoroge now lived contented without a single worry about tribal wars. They had a lot to thank the Europeans for.

Yes she did not like those politicians who came to corrupt the otherwise obedient and hard-working men, especially when

treated kindly. She did not like this murder of the Garstones. No!
She did not like it. And when she remembered the fact that she
was really alone, she thought it might be better for her to move
down to Nairobi or Kinangop and stay with friends a while. But
what would she do with her boys? Leave them there? She
wondered. She thought of Njoroge. A queer boy. Had he many
wives? Had he a large family? It was surprising even to her to
find that she had lived with him so long, yet had never thought of
these things. This reflection shocked her a little. It was the first
time she had ever thought of him as a man with a family. She
had always seen him as a servant. Even now it seemed ridiculous
to think of her houseboy as a father with a family. She sighed.
This was an omission, something to be righted in future.

And then she heard a knock on the front door and a voice
calling out 'Memsahib! Memsahib!'

It was Njoroge's voice. Her houseboy. Sweat broke out on
her face. She could not even hear what the boy was saying for the
circumstances of the Garstones' death came to her. This was her
end. The end of the road. So Njoroge had led them here! She
trembled and felt weak.

But suddenly, strength came back to her. She knew she was
alone. She knew they would break in. No! She would die
bravely. Holding her pistol more firmly in her hand, she opened
the door and quickly fired. Then a nausea came over her. She
had killed a man for the first time. She felt weak and fell down
crying, 'Come and kill me!' She did not know that she had in
fact killed her saviour.

On the following day, it was all in the papers. That a single
woman could fight a gang fifty strong was bravery unknown.
And to think she had killed one too!

Mrs Smiles and Mrs Hardy were especially profuse in their
congratulations.

'We told you they're all bad.'

'They are all bad,' agreed Mrs Hardy. Mrs Hill kept quiet.
The circumstances of Njoroge's death worried her. The more

she thought about it, the more of a puzzle it was to her. She gazed still into space. Then she let out a slow enigmatic sigh.

'I don't know,' she said.

'Don't know?' Mrs Hardy asked.

'Yes. That's it. Inscrutable.' Mrs Smiles was triumphant. 'All of them should be whipped.'

'All of them should be whipped,' agreed Mrs Hardy.

THE RETURN

The road was long. Whenever he took a step forward, little clouds of dust rose, whirled angrily behind him, and then slowly settled again. But a thin train of dust was left in the air, moving like smoke. He walked on, however, unmindful of the dust and ground under his feet. Yet with every step he seemed more and more conscious of the hardness and apparent animosity of the road. Not that he looked down; on the contrary, he looked straight ahead as if he would, any time now, see a familiar object that would hail him as a friend and tell him that he was near home. But the road stretched on.

He made quick, springing steps, his left hand dangling freely by the side of his once white coat, now torn and worn out. His right hand, bent at the elbow, held onto a string tied to a small bundle on his slightly drooping back. The bundle, well wrapped with a cotton cloth that had once been printed with red flowers now faded out, swung from side to side in harmony with the rhythm of his steps. The bundle held the bitterness and hardships of the years spent in detention camps. Now and then he looked at the sun on its homeward journey. Sometimes he darted quick side-glances at the small hedged strips of land which, with their sickly-looking crops, maize, beans, and peas, appeared much as everything else did – unfriendly. The whole country was dull and seemed weary. To Kamau, this was nothing new. He remembered that, even before the Mau Mau emergency, the over-tilled Gikuyu holdings wore haggard looks in contrast to the sprawling green fields in the settled area.

A path branched to the left. He hesitated for a moment and then made up his mind. For the first time, his eyes brightened a little as he went along the path that would take him down the

valley and then to the village. At last home was near and, with
that realization, the faraway look of a weary traveller seemed to
desert him for a while. The valley and the vegetation along it were
in deep contrast to the surrounding country. For here green
bush and trees thrived. This could only mean one thing: Honia
river still flowed. He quickened his steps as if he could scarcely
believe this to be true till he had actually set his eyes on the river.
It was there; it still flowed. Honia, where so often he had taken
a bathe, plunging stark naked into its cool living water, warmed
his heart as he watched its serpentine movement round the rocks
and heard its slight murmurs. A painful exhilaration passed all
over him, and for a moment he longed for those days. He sighed.
Perhaps the river would not recognize in his hardened features
that same boy to whom the riverside world had meant everything. Yet as he approached Honia, he felt more akin to it than
he had felt to anything else since his release.

A group of women were drawing water. He was excited, for
he could recognize one or two from his ridge. There was the
middle-aged Wanjiku, whose deaf son had been killed by the
Security Forces just before he himself was arrested. She had
always been a darling of the village, having a smile for everyone
and food for all. Would they receive him? Would they give him a
'hero's welcome'? He thought so. Had he not always been a
favourite all along the Ridge? And had he not fought for the
land? He wanted to run and shout: 'Here I am. I have come
back to you.' But he desisted. He was a man.

'Is it well with you?' A few voices responded. The other
women, with tired and worn features, looked at him mutely as if
his greeting was of no consequence. Why! Had he been so long
in the camp? His spirits were damped as he feebly asked:
'Do you not remember me?' Again they looked at him. They
stared at him with cold, hard looks; like everything else, they
seemed to be deliberately refusing to know or own him. It was
Wanjiku who at last recognized him. But there was neither
warmth nor enthusiasm in her voice as she said, 'Oh, is it you,

Kamau? We thought you—' She did not continue. Only now he noticed something else – surprise? fear? He could not tell. He saw their quick glances dart at him and he knew for certain that a secret from which he was excluded bound them together.

'Perhaps I am no longer one of them!' he bitterly reflected. But they told him of the new village. The old village of scattered huts spread thinly over the Ridge was no more.

He left them, feeling embittered and cheated. The old village had not even waited for him. And suddenly he felt a strong nostalgia for his old home, friends and surroundings. He thought of his father, mother and – and – he dared not think about her. But for all that, Muthoni, just as she had been in the old days, came back to his mind. His heart beat faster. He felt desire and a warmth thrilled through him. He quickened his step. He forgot the village women as he remembered his wife. He had stayed with her for a mere two weeks; then he had been swept away by the Colonial Forces. Like many others, he had been hurriedly screened and then taken to detention without trial. And all that time he had thought of nothing but the village and his beautiful woman.

The others had been like him. They had talked of nothing but their homes. One day he was working next to another detainee from Muranga. Suddenly the detainee, Njoroge, stopped breaking stones. He sighed heavily. His worn-out eyes had a faraway look.

'What's wrong, man? What's the matter with you?' Kamau asked.

'It is my wife. I left her expecting a baby. I have no idea what has happened to her.'

Another detainee put in: 'For me, I left my woman with a baby. She had just been delivered. We were all happy. But on the same day, I was arrested . . .'

And so they went on. All of them longed for one day – the day of their return home. Then life would begin anew.

Kamau himself had left his wife without a child. He had not
even finished paying the bride-price. But now he would go, seek
work in Nairobi, and pay off the remainder to Muthoni's parents.
Life would indeed begin anew. They would have a son and bring
him up in their own home. With these prospects before his eyes,
he quickened his steps. He wanted to run – no, fly to hasten his
return. He was now nearing the top of the hill. He wished he
could suddenly meet his brothers and sisters. Would they ask
him questions? He would, at any rate, not tell them all: the
beating, the screening and the work on roads and in quarries with
an askari always nearby ready to kick him if he relaxed. Yes. He
had suffered many humiliations, and he had not resisted. Was
there any need? But his soul and all the vigour of his manhood
had rebelled and bled with rage and bitterness.

One day these wazungu would go!

One day his people would be free! Then, then – he did not
know what he would do. However, he bitterly assured himself
no one would ever flout his manhood again.

He mounted the hill and then stopped. The whole plain lay
below. The new village was before him – rows and rows of
compact mud huts, crouching on the plain under the fast-
vanishing sun. Dark blue smoke curled upwards from various
huts, to form a dark mist that hovered over the village. Beyond,
the deep, blood-red sinking sun sent out finger-like streaks of
light that thinned outwards and mingled with the grey mist
shrouding the distant hills.

In the village, he moved from street to street, meeting new
faces. He inquired. He found his home. He stopped at the entrance
to the yard and breathed hard and full. This was the moment of
his return home. His father sat huddled up on a three-legged
stool. He was now very aged and Kamau pitied the old man. But
he had been spared – yes, spared to see his son's return—

'Father!'

The old man did not answer. He just looked at Kamau with
strange vacant eyes. Kamau was impatient. He felt annoyed and

irritated. Did he not see him? Would he behave like the women
Kamau had met at the river?

In the street, naked and half-naked children were playing,
throwing dust at one another. The sun had already set and it
looked as if there would be moonlight.

'Father, don't you remember me?' Hope was sinking in him.
He felt tired. Then he saw his father suddenly start and tremble
like a leaf. He saw him stare with unbelieving eyes. Fear was
discernible in those eyes. His mother came, and his brothers too.
They crowded around him. His aged mother clung to him and
sobbed hard.

'I knew my son would come. I knew he was not dead.'

'Why, who told you I was dead?'

'That Karanja, son of Njogu.'

And then Kamau understood. He understood his trembling
father. He understood the women at the river. But one thing
puzzled him: he had never been in the same detention camp with
Karanja. Anyway he had come back. He wanted now to see
Muthoni. Why had she not come out? He wanted to shout, 'I
have come, Muthoni; I am here.' He looked around. His mother
understood him. She quickly darted a glance at her man and
then simply said:

'Muthoni went away'.

Kamau felt something cold settle in his stomach. He looked at
the village huts and the dullness of the land. He wanted to ask
many questions but he dared not. He could not yet believe that
Muthoni had gone. But he knew by the look of the women at the
river, by the look of his parents, that she was gone.

'She was a good daughter to us,' his mother was explaining.
'She waited for you and patiently bore all the ills of the land.
Then Karanja came and said that you were dead. Your father
believed him. She believed him too and keened for a month.
Karanja constantly paid us visits. He was of your Rika, you know.
Then she got a child. We could have kept her. But where is the
land? Where is the food? Ever since land consolidation, our last

security was taken away. We let Karanja go with her. Other
women have done worse – gone to town. Only the infirm and the
old have been left here.'

He was not listening; the coldness in his stomach slowly
changed to bitterness. He felt bitter against all, all the people
including his father and mother. They had betrayed him. They
had leagued against him, and Karanja had always been his rival.
Five years was admittedly not a short time. But why did she go?
Why did they allow her to go? He wanted to speak. Yes, speak
and denounce everything – the women at the river, the village
and the people who dwelt there. But he could not. This bitter
thing was choking him.

'You – you gave my own away?' he whispered.

'Listen, child, child—'

The big yellow moon dominated the horizon. He hurried
away bitter and blind, and only stopped when he came to the
Honia river.

And standing at the bank, he saw not the river, but his hopes
dashed on the ground instead. The river moved swiftly, making
ceaseless monotonous murmurs. In the forest the crickets and
other insects kept up an incessant buzz. And above, the moon
shone bright. He tried to remove his coat, and the small bundle
he had held on to so firmly fell. It rolled down the bank and
before Kamau knew what was happening, it was floating swiftly
down the river. For a time he was shocked and wanted to
retrieve it. What would he show his – Oh, had he forgotten so
soon? His wife had gone. And the little things that had so
strangely reminded him of her and that he had guarded all those
years, had gone! He did not know why, but somehow he felt
relieved. Thoughts of drowning himself dispersed. He began to
put on his coat, murmuring to himself, 'Why should she have
waited for me? Why should all the changes have waited for my
return?'

A MEETING IN THE DARK

He stood at the door of the hut and saw his old, frail but energetic father coming along the village street, with a rather dirty bag made out of a strong calico swinging by his side. His father always carried this bag. John knew what it contained: a Bible, a hymn-book and probably a notebook and a pen. His father was a preacher. He knew it was he who had stopped his mother from telling him stories when be became a man of God. His mother had stopped telling him stories long ago. She would say to him, 'Now, don't ask for any more stories. Your father may come.' So he feared his father. John went in and warned his mother of his father's coming. Then his father entered. John stood aside, then walked towards the door. He lingered there doubtfully, then he went out.

'John, hei, John!'

'Baba!'

'Come back.'

He stood doubtfully in front of his father. His heart beat faster and there was that anxious voice within him asking: Does he know?

'Sit down. Where are you going?'

'For a walk, Father,' he answered evasively.

'To the village?'

'Well-yes-no. I mean, nowhere in particular.' John saw his father look at him hard, seeming to read his face. John sighed, a very slow sigh. He did not like the way his father eyed him. He always looked at him as though John was a sinner, one who had to be watched all the time. 'I am,' his heart told him. John guiltily refused to meet the old man's gaze and looked past him appealingly to his mother who was quietly peeling potatoes. But she seemed oblivious of everything around her.

'Why do you look away? What have you done?'

John shrank within himself with fear. But his face remained expressionless. He could hear the loud beats of his heart. It was like an engine pumping water. He felt no doubt his father knew all about it. He thought: 'Why does he torture me? Why does he not at once say he knows?' Then another voice told him: 'No, he doesn't know, otherwise he would have already jumped at you.' A consolation. He faced his thoughtful father with courage.

'When is the journey?'

Again John thought: Why does he ask? I have told him many times.

'Next week, Tuesday,' he said.

'Right. Tomorrow we go to the shops, hear?'

'Yes, Father.'

'Then be prepared.'

'Yes, Father.'

'You can go.'

'Thank you, Father.' He began to move.

'John!'

'Yes?' John's heart almost stopped beating.

'You seem to be in a hurry. I don't want to hear of you loitering in the village. I know young men, going to show off just because you are going away? I don't want to hear of trouble in the village.'

Much relieved, he went out. He could guess what his father meant by not wanting trouble in the village.

'Why do you persecute the boy so much?' Susana spoke for the first time. Apparently she had carefully listened to the whole drama without a word. Now was her time to speak. She looked at her tough old preacher who had been a companion for life. She had married him a long time ago. She could not tell the number of years. They had been happy. Then the man became a convert. And everything in the home put on a religious tone.

He even made her stop telling stories to the child. 'Tell him of Jesus. Jesus died for you. Jesus died for the child. He must know the Lord.' She, too, had been converted. But she was never blind to the moral torture he inflicted on the boy (that was how she always referred to John), so that the boy had grown up mortally afraid of his father. She always wondered if it was love for the son. Or could it be a resentment because, well, they two had 'sinned' before marriage? John had been the result of that sin. But that had not been John's fault. It was the boy who ought to complain. She often wondered if the boy had ... but no. The boy had been very small when they left Fort Hall. She looked at her husband. He remained mute though his left hand did, rather irritably, feel about his face.

'It is as if he was not your son. Or do you ...'

'Hm, Sister.' The voice was pleading. She was seeking a quarrel but he did not feel equal to one. Really, women could never understand. Women were women, whether saved or not. Their son had to be protected against all evil influences. He must be made to grow in the footsteps of the Lord. He looked at her, frowning a little. She had made him sin but that had been a long time ago. And he had been saved. John must not tread the same road.

'You ought to tell us to leave. You know I can go away. Go back to Fort Hall. And then everybody ...'

'Look, Sister,' he hastily interrupted. He always called her sister. Sister-in-Lord, in full. But he sometimes wondered if she had been truly saved. In his heart he prayed: Lord, be with our sister Susana. Aloud, he continued, 'You know I want the boy to grow in the Lord.'

'But you torture him so! You make him fear you!'

'Why! He should not fear me. I have really nothing against him.'

'It is you. You. You have always been cruel to him ...' She stood up. The peelings dropped from her frock and fell in a heap on the floor. 'Stanley!'

'Sister.' He was startled by the vehemence in her voice. He had never seen her like this. Lord, take the devil out of her. Save her this minute. She did not say what she wanted to say. Stanley looked away from her. It was a surprise, but it seemed he feared his wife. If you had told the people in the village about this, they would not have believed you. He took his Bible and began to read. On Sunday he would preach to a congregation of brethren and sisters.

Susana, a rather tall, thin woman, who had once been beautiful, sat down again and went on with her work. She did not know what was troubling her son. Was it the coming journey? Still, she feared for him.

Outside, John was strolling aimlessly along the path that led from his home. He stood near the wattle tree which was a little way from his father's house and surveyed the whole village. They lay before his eyes, crammed, rows and rows of mud and grass huts, ending in sharply defined sticks that pointed to heaven. Smoke was coming out of various huts. It was an indication that many women had already come from the shambas. Night would soon fall. To the west, the sun – that lone day-time traveller – was hurrying home behind the misty hills. Again, John looked at the crammed rows and rows of huts that formed Makeno Village, one of the new mushroom 'towns' that grew up all over the country during the Mau Mau war. It looked so ugly. A pain rose in his heart and he felt like crying – I hate you, I hate you! You trapped me alive. Away from you, it would never have happened. He did not shout. He just watched.

A woman was coming towards where he stood. A path into the village was just near there. She was carrying a big load of Kuni which bent her into an Akamba-bow shape. She greeted him. 'Is it well with you, Njooni (John)?'

'It is well with me, Mother.' There was no trace of bitterness in his voice. John was by nature polite. Everyone knew this. He was quite unlike the other proud, educated sons of the tribe – sons who came back from the other side of the waters with white or Negro wives who spoke English. And they behaved just like Europeans! John was a favourite, a model of humility and moral perfection. Everyone knew that though a clergyman's son, John would never betray the tribe. They still talked of the tribe and its ways.

'When are you going to – to—'

'Makerere?'

'Makelele.' She laughed. The way she pronounced the name was funny. And the way she laughed, too. She enjoyed it. But John felt hurt. So everyone knew of this.

'Next week.'

'I wish you well.'

'Thank you, Mother.'

She said quietly, as if trying to pronounce it better 'Makelele'. She laughed at herself again but she was tired. The load was heavy.

'Stay well, Son.'

'Go well and in peace, Mother.'

And the woman who all the time had stood, moved on, panting like a donkey, but she was obviously pleased with John's politeness.

John remained long, looking at her. What made such a woman live on day to day, working hard, yet happy? Had she much faith in life? Or was her faith in the tribe? She and her kind, who had never been touched by ways of the whiteman, looked as though they had something to cling to. As he watched her disappear, he felt proud that they should think well of him. He felt proud that he had a place in their esteem. And then came the pang. *Father will know. They will know.* He did not know what he feared most; the action his father would take when he found out, or the loss of the little faith the simple villagers had placed in him, when they knew. He feared to lose everything.

He went down to the small local tea-shop. He met many people who wished him well at the college. All of them knew that the priest's son had finished all the whiteman's learning in Kenya.

He would now go to Uganda. They had read this in the *Baraza*, the Swahili Weekly. John did not stay long at the shop. The sun had already gone to rest and now darkness was coming. The evening meal was ready. His tough father was still at the table reading his Bible. He did not look up when John entered. Strange silence settled in the hut.

'You look unhappy.' His mother first broke the silence.

John laughed. It was a nervous little laugh. 'No, Mother,' he hastily replied, nervously looking at his father. He secretly hoped that Wamuhu had not blabbed.

'Then I am glad.'

She did not know. He ate his dinner and went out to his hut. A man's hut. Every young man had his own hut. John was never allowed to bring any girl visitor in there. Stanley did not want 'trouble'. Even to be seen standing with one was a crime. His father could easily thrash him. He feared his father, though sometimes he wondered why he feared him. He ought to have rebelled like the other educated young men. He lit the lantern. He took it in his hand. The yellow light flickered dangerously and then went out. He knew his hands were shaking. He lit it again and hurriedly took his big coat and a huge Kofia which were lying on the unmade bed. He left the lantern burning, so that his father would see it and think he was in. John bit his lower lip spitefully. He hated himself for being so girlish. It was unnatural for a boy of his age.

Like a shadow, he stealthily crossed the courtyard and went on to the village street.

He met young men and women lining the streets. They were laughing, talking, whispering. They were obviously enjoying themselves. John thought, they are more free than I am. He envied their exuberance. They clearly stood outside or above the strict morality that the educated ones had to be judged by. Would he have gladly changed places with them? He wondered. At last, he came to the hut. It stood at the very heart of the village. How well he knew it – to his sorrow. He wondered what he should do! Wait for her outside? What if her mother came out instead? He decided to enter.

'Hodi!'

'Enter. We are in.'

John pulled down his hat before he entered. Indeed they were all there – all except she whom he wanted. The fire in the hearth was dying. Only a small flame from a lighted lantern vaguely illuminated the whole hut. The flame and the giant shadow created on the wall seemed to be mocking him. He prayed that Wamuhu's parents would not recognize him. He tried to be 'thin', and to disguise his voice as he greeted them. They recognized him and made themselves busy on his account. To be visited by such an educated one, who knew all about the whiteman's world and knowledge and who would now go to another land beyond, was not such a frequent occurrence that it could be taken lightly. Who knew but he might be interested in their daughter? Stranger things had happened. After all, learning was not the only thing. Though Wamuhu had no learning, yet she had charms and could be trusted to captivate any young man's heart with her looks and smiles.

'You will sit down. Take that stool.'

'No!' He noticed with bitterness that he did not call her 'Mother'.

'Where is Wamuhu?'

The mother threw a triumphant glance at her husband. They exchanged a knowing look. John bit his lip again and felt like bolting. He controlled himself with difficulty.

'She has gone out to get some tea leaves. Please sit down. She will cook you some tea when she comes.'

'I am afraid . . .' he muttered some inaudible words and went out. He almost collided with Wamuhu.

In the hut: 'Didn't I tell you? Trust a woman's eye!'

'You don't know these young men.'

'But you see John is different. Everyone speaks well of him and he is a clergyman's son.'

'Y-e-e-s! A clergyman's son! You forget your daughter is circumcised.' The old man was remembering his own day. He had found for himself a good virtuous woman, initiated in all the tribe's ways. And she had known no other man. He had married her. They were happy. Other men of his Rika had done the same. All the girls had been virgins, it being a taboo to touch a girl in that way, even if you slept in the same bed, as indeed so many young men and girls did. Then the white men had come, preaching a strange religion, strange ways, which all men followed. The tribe's code of behaviour was broken. The new faith could not keep the tribe together. How could it? The men who followed the new faith would not let the girls be circumcised. And they would not let their sons marry circumcised girls. Puu! Look at what was happening. Their young men went away to the land of the whitemen. What did they bring? White women. Black women who spoke English. Aaa – bad. And the young men who were left just did not mind. They made unmarried girls their wives and then left them with fatherless children.

'What does it matter?' his wife was replying. 'Is Wamuhu not as good as the best of them? Anyway, John is different.'

'Different! Different! Puu! They are all alike. Those coated with the white clay of the whiteman's ways are the worst. They have nothing inside. Nothing – nothing here.' He took a piece of wood and nervously poked the dying fire. A strange numbness came over him. He trembled. And he feared; he feared for the tribe. For now he saw it was not only the educated men who were coated with strange ways, but the whole tribe. The old man trembled and cried inside mourning for a tribe that had crumbled. The tribe had nowhere to go to. And it could not be what it was before. He stopped poking and looked hard at the ground.

'I wonder why he came. I wonder.' Then he looked at his wife and said, 'Have you seen strange behaviour with your daughter?'

His wife did not answer. She was preoccupied with her own great hopes.

John and Wamuhu walked on in silence. The intricate streets

and turns were well known to them both. Wamuhu walked with quick light steps; John knew she was in a happy mood. His steps were heavy and he avoided people, even though it was dark. But why should he feel ashamed? The girl was beautiful, probably the most beautiful girl in the whole of Limuru. Yet he feared being seen with her. It was all wrong. He knew that he could have loved her; even then he wondered if he did not love her. Perhaps it was hard to tell but, had he been one of the young men he had met, he would not have hesitated in his answer.

Outside the village he stopped. She, too, stopped. Neither had spoken a word all through. Perhaps the silence spoke louder than words. Both of them were only too conscious of each other.

'Do they know?' Silence. Wamuhu was probably considering the question. 'Don't keep me waiting. Please answer me,' he implored. He felt weary, very weary, like an old man who had suddenly reached his journey's end.

'No. You told me to give you one more week. A week is over today.'

'Yes. That's why I came!' John whispered hoarsely.

Wamuhu did not speak. John looked at her. Darkness was now between them. He was not really seeing her; before him was the image of his father – haughtily religious and dominating. Again he thought: I, John, a priest's son, respected by all and going to college, will fall, fall to the ground. He did not want to contemplate the fall.

'It was your fault.' He found himself accusing her. In his heart he knew he was lying.

'Why do you keep on telling me that? Don't you want to marry me?'

John sighed. He did not know what to do. He remembered a story his mother used to tell him. *Once upon a time there was a young girl . . . she had no home to go to and she could not go forward to the beautiful land and see all the good things because the Irimu was on the way . . .*

'When will you tell them?'

'Tonight.'

He felt desperate. Next week he would go to the college. If he could persuade her to wait, he might be able to get away and come back when the storm and consternation had abated. But then the government might withdraw his bursary. He was frightened and there was a sad note of appeal as he turned to her and said, 'Look, Wamuhu, how long have you been pre-... I mean, like this?'

'I have told you over and over again, I have been pregnant for three months and mother is being suspicious. Only yesterday she said I breathed like a woman with a child.'

'Do you think you could wait for three weeks more?'

She laughed. Ah! the little witch! She knew his trick. Her laughter always aroused many emotions in him.

'All right,' he said. 'Give me just tomorrow. I'll think up something. Tomorrow I'll let you know.'

'I agree. Tomorrow. I cannot wait any more unless you mean to marry me.'

Why not marry her? She is beautiful! Why not marry? Do I love her or don't I?

She left. John felt as if she was deliberately blackmailing him. His knees were weak and lost strength. He could not move but sank on the ground in a heap. Sweat poured profusely down his cheeks, as if he had been running hard under a strong sun. But this was cold sweat. He lay on the grass; he did not want to think. Oh, no! He could not possibly face his father. Or his mother. Or Reverend Carstone who had had such faith in him. John realized that, though he was educated, he was no more secure than anybody else. He was no better than Wamuhu. Then why don't you marry her? He did not know. John had grown up under a Calvinistic father and learnt under a Calvinistic headmaster – a missionary! John tried to pray. But to whom was he praying? To Carstone's God? It sounded false. It was as if he was blaspheming. Could he pray to the God of the tribe? His sense of guilt crushed him.

He woke up. Where was he? Then he understood. Wamuhu had left him. She had given him one day. He stood up; he felt good. Weakly, he began to walk back home. It was lucky that darkness blanketed the whole earth and him in it. From the various huts, he could hear laughter, heated talks or quarrels. Little fires could be seen flickering red through the open doors. Village stars, John thought. He raised up his eyes. The heavenly stars, cold and distant, looked down on him impersonally. Here and there, groups of boys and girls could be heard laughing and shouting. For them life seemed to go on as usual. John consoled himself by thinking that they, too, would come to face their day of trial.

John was shaky. Why! Why could he not defy all expectations, all prospects of a future, and marry the girl? No. No. It was impossible. She was circumcised and he knew that his father and the church would never consent to such a marriage. She had no learning – or rather she had not gone beyond standard four. Marrying her would probably ruin his chances of ever going to a university.

He tried to move briskly. His strength had returned. His imagination and thought took flight. He was trying to explain his action before an accusing world – he had done so many times before, ever since he knew of this. He still wondered what he could have done. The girl had attracted him. She was graceful and her smile had been very bewitching. There was none who could equal her and no girl in the village had any pretence to any higher standard of education. Women's education was very low. Perhaps that was why so many Africans went 'away' and came back married. He too wished he had gone with the others, especially in the last giant student airlift to America. If only Wamuhu had learning ... and she was uncircumcised ... then he might probably rebel.

The light still shone in his mother's hut. John wondered if he should go in for the night prayers. But he thought against it; he might not be strong enough to face his parents. In his hut the light had gone out. He hoped his father had not noticed it.

John woke up early. He was frightened. He was normally not superstitious, but still he did not like the dreams of the night. He dreamt of circumcision; he had just been initiated in the tribal manner. Somebody – he could not tell his face, came and led him because he took pity on him. They went, went into a strange land. Somehow, he found himself alone. The somebody had vanished. A ghost came. He recognized it as the ghost of the home he had left. It pulled him back; then another ghost came. It was the ghost of the land he had come to. It pulled him forward. The two contested. Then came other ghosts from all sides and pulled him from all sides so that his body began to fall into pieces. And the ghosts were insubstantial. He could not cling to any. Only they were pulling him and he was becoming nothing, nothing ... he was now standing a distance away. It had not been him. But he was looking at the girl, the girl in the story. She had nowhere to go. He thought he would go to help her; he would show her the way. But as he went to her, he lost his way ... he was all alone ... something destructive was coming towards him, coming, coming ... He woke up. He was sweating all over.

Dreams about circumcision were no good. They portended death. He dismissed the dream with a laugh. He opened the window only to find the whole country clouded in mist. It was perfect July weather in Limuru. The hills, ridges, valleys and plains that surrounded the village were lost in the mist. It looked such a strange place. But there was almost a magic fascination in it. Limuru was a land of contrasts and evoked differing emotions at different times. Once John would be fascinated and would yearn to touch the land, embrace it or just be on the grass. At another time he would feel repelled by the dust, the strong sun and the pot-holed roads. If only his struggle were just against the dust, the mist, the sun and the rain, he might feel content. Content to live here. At least he thought he would never like to die and be buried anywhere else but at Limuru. But there was the human element whose vices and betrayal of other men were embodied in the new ugly villages. The last night's incident rushed into his mind like a flood, making him weak again. He got out of his blankets and went out. Today he would go to the shops. He was uneasy. An odd feeling was coming to him – in fact had been coming – that his relationship with his father was perhaps unnatural. But he dismissed the thought. Tonight would be the day of reckoning. He shuddered to think of it. It was unfortunate that this scar had come into his life at this time, when he was going to Makerere and it would have brought him closer to his father.

They went to the shops. All day long, John remained quiet as they moved from shop to shop buying things from the lanky but wistful Indian traders. And all day long, John wondered why he feared his father so much. He had grown up fearing him, trembling whenever he spoke or gave commands. John was not alone in this.

Stanley was feared by all.

He preached with great vigour, defying the very gates of hell. Even during the Emergency, he had gone on preaching, scolding, judging and condemning. All those who were not saved were destined for hell. Above all, Stanley was known for his great and strict moral observances – a bit too strict, rather pharisaical in nature. None noticed this; certainly not the sheep he shepherded. If an elder broke any of the rules, he was liable to be expelled, or excommunicated. Young men and women, seen standing together 'in a manner prejudicial to church and God's morality' (they were one anyway) were liable to be excommunicated. And so, many young men tried to serve two masters by seeing their girls at night and going to church by day. The alternative was to give up church-going altogether.

Stanley took a fatherly attitude to all the people in the village. You must be strict with what is yours. And because of all this he wanted his house to be a good example of this to all. That is why he wanted his son to grow upright. But motives behind many human actions may be mixed. He could never forget that he had also fallen before his marriage. Stanley was also a product of the disintegration of the tribe due to the new influences.

The shopping did not take long. His father strictly observed the silences between them and neither by word nor by hint did he refer to last night. They reached home and John was thinking that all was well when his father called him.

'John.'

'Yes, Father.'

'Why did you not come for prayers last night?'

'I forgot . . .'

'Where were you?'

Why do you ask me? What right have you to know where I was? One day I am going to revolt against you. But, immediately, John knew that this act of rebellion was something beyond him – unless something happened to push him into it. It needed someone with something he lacked.

'I – I – I mean, I was . . .'

'You should not sleep so early before prayers. Remember to turn up tonight.'

'I will.'

Something in the boy's voice made the father look up. John went away relieved. All was still well.

Evening came. John dressed like the night before and walked with faltering steps towards the fatal place. The night of reckoning had come. And he had not thought of anything. After this night all would know. Even Reverend Carstone would hear of it. He remembered Reverend Carstone and the last words of blessing he had spoken to him. No! he did not want to remember. It was no good remembering these things; and yet the words came. They were clearly written in the air, or in the darkness of his mind. 'You are going into the world. The world is waiting even like a hungry lion, to swallow you, to devour you. Therefore, beware of the world. Jesus said, Hold fast unto . . .' John felt a pain – a pain that wriggled through his flesh as he remembered these words. He contemplated the coming fall. Yes! He, John, would fall from the Gates of Heaven down through the open waiting Gates of Hell. Ah! He could see it all, and all that people would say. All would shun his company, all would give him oblique looks that told so much. The trouble with John was that his imagination magnified the fall from the heights of 'goodness' out of all proportion. And fear of people and consequences ranked high in the things that made him contemplate the fall with so much horror.

John devised all sorts of punishment for himself. And when it came to thinking of a way out, only fantastic and impossible ways of escape came into his head. He simply could not make up his mind. And because he could not, and because he feared Father and people and did not know his true attitude to the girl, he came to the agreed spot having nothing to tell her. Whatever he did looked fatal to him. Then suddenly he said:

'Look, Wamuhu. Let me give you money. You might then say that someone else was responsible. Lots of girls have done this. Then that man may marry you. For me, it is impossible. You know that.'

'No. I cannot do that. How can you, you . . .'

'I will give you two hundred shillings.'

'No!'

'Three hundred.'

'No!' She was almost crying. It pained her to see him so.

'Four hundred, five hundred, six hundred.' John had begun calmly but now his voice was running high. He was excited. He was becoming more desperate. Did he know what he was talking about? He spoke quickly, breathlessly, as if he was in a hurry. The figure was rapidly rising – nine thousand, ten thousand, twenty thousand . . . He is mad. He is foaming. He is quickly moving towards the girl in the dark. He has lain his hands on her shoulders and is madly imploring her in a hoarse voice. Deep inside him, something horrid that assumes the threatening anger of his father and the village seems to be pushing him. He is violently shaking Wamuhu, while his mind tells him that he is patting her gently. Yes, he is out of his mind. The figure has now reached fifty thousand shillings and is increasing. Wamuhu is afraid. She extricates herself from him, the mad, educated son of a religious clergyman, and runs. He runs after her and holds her, calling her by all sorts of endearing words. But he is shaking her, shake, shake, her, her – he tries to hug her by the neck, presses. ... She lets out one horrible scream and then falls on the ground. And so all of a sudden, the struggle is over, the figures stop, and John stands there trembling like the leaf of a tree on a windy day.

Soon everyone will know that he has created and then killed.

GOODBYE AFRICA

She was in the kitchen making coffee. She loved making coffee even in the daytime when the servants were around. The smell of real coffee soothed her. Besides, the kitchen was a world to her. Her husband never went in there.

He was now in the sitting room, and to him the noise from the disturbed crockery seemed to issue from another land. He picked a book from the glass-fronted shelf. He sat down on the sofa, opened the book at random, but did not read it. He just let it drop beside him.

She came in, holding a wooden tray with both hands. She enjoyed the feel of things made from wood. She put the tray on a table at the corner of the room. Then she arranged side tables, one for him and the other for herself. She sat down to her coffee, facing him. She saw his look was fixed past her. He did not seem to have noticed his cup of coffee. She stood up as if to go to him. But instead she picked up a tiny piece of paper on the floor and sat down again. She liked her house to be specklessly clean.

'The thought of leaving didn't bother me until tonight,' she said, and knew it was not true. She felt the triteness of her comment and kept quiet.

He avoided her look and now played with the cup. He thought about everything and nothing. Suddenly, he felt bitter: why did she judge him all the time? Why couldn't she at least speak out her silent accusations?

And she thought he must also be sad at leaving. Fifteen years is not a small period of one's life and God, I don't make it easy for him. She was filled with sudden compassion. She made sweet, pious resolutions. I'll try to understand him. For a start, I'll open my heart to him, tonight. Now she walked up to his side, placed her left hand on his shoulder: 'Come to bed, you must be tired, all that noise at the party.'

He put down his cup and patted the hand on his shoulder, before removing it gently. 'Go. I'll soon join you.' She felt a suggestion of impatience in his voice. And he was angry because his hand was not steady.

My hands are losing their firmness, he was thinking. Or did I drink too much? No, my hand suddenly became weak, so weak. She was laughing at me. Was it my fault, what, what fault? I didn't mean to do it. I couldn't have meant it, he insisted harder now addressing himself to his absent wife. He drove me into it, he whispered uncertainly, going to the low cupboard by the wall, and taking out the only remaining bottle of whisky. Scotch, Johnny Walker born 1840 and still walking strong. He laughed a little. He poured himself a glass, and gulped it down, poured another, drank and then went back to the seat keeping the bottle beside him. Why then should a thing that never happened – well – perhaps it did happen, but he never meant it – how could it come to trouble him?

He had forgotten about the incident until these, his last months in Africa. Then he had started re-enacting the scene in his dreams, the vision becoming more and more vivid as days and months whistled by. At first the face had only appeared to him by night. His bed held terror for him. Then suddenly, these last few days, the face started appearing before him in broad daylight. Why didn't he get visitations from all the other Mau Mau terrorists he had tortured and killed? Except the man, that!

Yet he knew the man was not like the others. This man had worked for him as a shamba boy. A nice, God-fearing, sub-missive boy. A model of his type. He loved the boy and often gave him presents. Old shoes, old clothes. Things like that. He remembered the gratitude in the boy's face and his gestures of appreciation, a little comic perhaps, and it had made giving them worthwhile. It was this feeling of doing something for the people here that made the things you had to put up with bearable. Here in Africa you felt you were doing something tangible, something that was immediately appreciated. Not like in Europe where nobody seemed to care what you did, where even the poor in the East of London refused to seize opportunities offered them. The Welfare State. G-r-r-r-r! Such thoughts had made him feel that the boy was more than a servant. He felt somehow fatherly towards him ... responsible, and the boy was his. Then one Christmas, the boy suddenly threw back at him the gift of a long coat and ten shillings. The boy had laughed and walked out of his service. For a long time, he could never forget the laughter. This he could have forgiven. But the grief and the misery in his wife's face at the news of the boy's disappearance was something else. For this he could never forgive the boy. Later when the Mau Mau War broke out, he, as a screening officer, was to meet the boy.

He drank steadily as if in vengeance for years of abstinence and outward respectability. The ceiling, the floor, the chairs swam in the air. I'll be all right if I go for a drive, for a small drive, he suggested to himself, and staggered out daring the man to appear before him with that sneering laughter.

He got into the car. The headlights swept away the darkness. He did not know where he was going, he just abandoned himself to the road. Sometimes he would recognize a familiar tree or a signpost then he would go into a blackout and drive blindly. In this way, dozing, waking, telling himself to hold on to the steering wheel, he swerved round sharp corners and bends, down the valley, avoiding, miraculously, one or two vehicles from the opposite direction. What am I doing? I am mad, he muttered and unexpectedly swerved to the right, leaving the road, and just managing to avoid crashing into a passing train at the crossing. He drove through the grass into the forest; he hit into bumps, brushed against tree stumps, again miraculously avoided hitting the tree trunks. I must stop this, he thought, and to prove that he had not yet lost his head, he braked the car to a sudden standstill.

He had heard of rituals in the dark. He had even read

somewhere that some of the early European settlers used to go to
African sorcerers, to have curses lifted. He had considered these
things opposed to reason: but what had happened to him, the
visions, surely worked against the normal laws of reason. No,
he would exorcise the hallucinations from his system, here, in the
dark. The idea was attractive and, in his condition, irresistible.
Africa does this to you, he thought as he stripped himself naked.
He now staggered out of the car and walked a little distance into
the forest. Darkness and the forest buzzing crept around him. He
was afraid, but he stood his ground. What next? He did not
know anything about African magic. At home he had heard
vague things like faerie folk, rowan trees, stolen babies and
kelpies. He had heard, or read, that you could make waxen
images of somebody you wanted to harm and at the dead of the
night stick pins into the eyes. Maybe he ought to do this; he
would make an image of that man, his former shamba boy, and
prick his eyes. Then he remembered that he had not brought any
wax and danced with fury, alone in the forest.

No, that'll never do, he thought, now ashamed of things of the
dark. I want to know what went wrong that even my wife laughs
at me. He went back to the car, hoping to find out why things in
Kenya, everywhere, were falling, falling apart. He had never
thought a day would come when a government would retire him
and replace him with a black. The shame of it. And his wife
looking at him with those eyes. Another idea more irresistible
than the first now possessed him. I'll write to her. I'll write to the
world. He fished out a notebook and started writing furiously.
Inspiration already made him feel light and buoyant within. The
light in the car dimly lit the pages, but he did not mind, because
words, ideas, were all in his head, he butchered his life and tried
to examine it, at the same time defending himself before her,
before the world.

. . . I know you have seen me shake before that face. You have
refused to comment, perhaps not to hurt me. But you laughed

at me all the time, didn't you? Don't deny it. I've seen it in your eyes and looks. I know you think me a failure. I never rose beyond the rank of Senior D.O. Africa has ruined me, but I never got a chance, really. Oh, don't look at me with those blue eyes as if you thought I lied. Maybe you are saying there's a tide in the affairs of men. O.K. I neglected it. We neglected it. But what tide? Oh, I am tired.

He stopped and read over what he had written. He turned over another page. Inspiration came in waves. His hand was too slow for what begged to come out.

. . . What went wrong, I keep on asking myself? Was it wrong for us, with our capital, with our knowledge, with our years of Christian civilization to open and lift a dark country onto the stage of history? I played my part. Does it matter if promotion was slow? Does it matter if there were ups and downs? And there were many moments of despair. I remember the huts we burnt. Even then I did ask myself: had I fallen so low? My life reduced to burning down huts and yet more huts? Had my life come to a cul-de-sac? And yet we could not let atavistic violence destroy all that had taken so many years and so many lives to build. When I had reached the nadir of my despair, I met that man – our shamba boy. Do you remember him? The one who spurned my gift and disappeared, maybe to the forest? He stood in the office with that sneer in his face – like – like the devil. The servile submissive face when he worked for you had gone. He had that strange effect on me – when I remembered the grief he caused you – well – made me boil inside – I felt a violent rage within such as I had never felt before – I could not bear that grin. I stood and spat into his face. And that arrogant stare never left his face even as he cleared off the spit with the back of his left hand. Isn't it strange that I forget his name now, that I never really knew his name? Did you? I only remember that he was tall and there in the office I saw the violence in his eyes. I was afraid of him. Can you believe it? I, afraid of a black man? Afraid of my former shamba boy? What happened later, I cannot remember, I cannot explain, I was not myself, I only saw the face of the man. At night, in the morning, I saw the grin, the sneer, the arrogant indifference. And he would not confess to anything. I gave command. He was taken to the forest. I never saw him again . . .

He wrote in fury; images flowed, merged, clashed: it was as if he had a few days to live and he wanted to purge his soul of something. A confession to a priest before the gallows fell. He was now shivering. But he was still possessed . . . I'm writing this to you, I am alone in the forest, and in the world. I want to begin a new life with you in England, after saying goodbye to Africa. . . . And now he discovered he had no clothes and that he was shivering. He felt ashamed of his nakedness and quickly put on his clothes. But he could not continue with his confession and he feared to read it over in case he changed his mind. He was now almost sober, but very excited at the prospect of giving his life to her, tonight.

She was not yet asleep. She too was determined to wait for him to come back so that they could share their last night in Africa. In bed, she allowed her mind to glance backwards over her life, over her relationship with him. At first, in their early days in Kenya, she had tried to be enthusiastic about his civilizing zeal and his ambitions. She too was determined to play her part, to give life a purpose. She attended a few meetings of African women in the ridges and even learnt a smattering of Swahili. Then she wanted to understand Africa, to touch the centre, and feel the huge continent throb on her fingers. In those days she and he were close, their hearts seemed to beat together. But with the passage of years, he had gone farther and farther away. She lost her original enthusiasm: the ideas that had earlier appeared so bright faded and became rusty in her eyes. Who were they to civilize anyone? What was civilization anyway? And why did he fret because he could not climb up the ladder as quickly as he wanted? She became slightly impatient with this rusty thing that took him away from her, but she would not disturb him, ruin his career. So she went to the parties, did her share of small talk, and wanted to cry. Ought she to have spoken, then, she wondered now, wriggling in bed, puzzled by his late night drive. She gave up meetings in the villages. She wanted to be alone. She did not want to understand Africa. Why should she? She had not tried to understand Europe, or Australia where she was born. No. You could never hope to embrace the meaning of a continent in your small palms, you could only love. She wanted to live her own life, and not as a prop to another's climb to a top that promised no fuller life.

So she went for walks alone in the countryside: she saw children playing and wondered what it would feel like to have a child. When would her first arrive in this strange world? She was awed by the thick crowds of banana plants, the thick bush and forests. That was just before the Emergency when you could walk down alone anywhere without fear.

It was during one of her walks that the boy had first made love to her among the banana plantations. Freedom. And afterward their fevered love-making had finally severed her from the world of her husband and other District Officers.

Arriving home, he found she was not yet asleep. He went towards her, riding on low exciting waves. He did not put on the light but sat on the bed without speaking.

'Where have you been?'

'I went for a drive – seeing the old place for the last time.'

'Come into bed then, God, how cold you are! And here I was waiting for you to give me warmth.'

'You know it's always chilly at night.'

'Come on then'.

She felt she had to tell him now in the dark, about her lover. She did not want to look into his face in case she changed her mind. She put out her hand and stroked his head, feeling for a way to start. Now. Her heart was beating. Was she scared?

'I want to tell you something,' she removed her hand from his head, and paused, the next words refusing to come out. 'Will you forgive me?'

'Of course I will, everything.' He was impatient. What could she tell him greater than what he had written, red-hot, filling the notebook. He wanted to tell her how he had exorcised the ghost of the shamba boy from his life. He waited hoping she would finish quickly. He meant to give her the notebook and withdraw to the bathroom to give her time to see his bare soul.

'Of course I can forgive you anything,' he said by way of encouragement. 'Go on,' he whispered gently into the dark room.

She told him about the shamba boy – her lover.

He listened and felt energy and blood leave his body.

Would he forgive her? She only wanted them to start a new life. She finished, her voice fading into dark silence. She listened to her heart-beat waiting for him to speak.

But he did not speak. A kind of dullness had crept into his limbs, into his mouth, into the heart. The man. His shamba boy. For an answer he stood up and started toward the door.

'Darling, please!' She called out, for the first time feeling dark terror at his lack of words. 'Don't go. It was long way back, before the Emergency.'

But he continued walking, out through the door, into the sitting room. He sat on the sofa exactly where he had earlier. Automatically, he started fingering the unfinished cup of coffee.

For all his visions of moral ideals in the service of British capitalism, he was a vain man: he never really saw himself in any light but that of an adequate husband. He had no cause, within himself, to doubt her fidelity to him as a man, or a husband. How then could this woman, his wife, bring herself to sleep with that

man, that creature? How make herself so cheap, drag his
thousand-year-old name to mud, and such mud?

He had followed a dream for too long. He would not let the
dream go despite the reality around him. In his colonizing mission and his zeal to reach the top he had neglected his house and
another had occupied it. In this, perhaps, he was not alone. But
how could he know this as he sat in the middle of the room, the
bare walls staring at him? The cup fell out of his hands and
broke into pieces. He stood up and walked around the room,
slowly, looking at nothing, seeing neither yesterday nor tomorrow. Then he took out his notebook and opened it at
random:

> The white man in Africa must accept a more stringent moral
> code in the family and in the society at large. For we must set
> the ideals to which our African subjects must aspire.

He closed the notebook and walked into the kitchen where
he never went before. He took a match, struck it, and watched
the notebook burn. He watched the flame, saw his flesh burn,
but he felt no pain, nothing. The man's ghost would forever
pursue him. Africa.

PART III

PART III
Secret Lives

MINUTES OF GLORY

Her name was Wanjiru. But she liked better her Christian one, Beatrice. It sounded more pure and more beautiful. Not that she was ugly; but she could not be called beautiful either. Her body, dark and full fleshed, had the form, yes, but it was as if it waited to be filled by the spirit. She worked in beer halls where sons of women came to drown their inner lives in beer cans and froth. Nobody seemed to notice her. Except, perhaps, when a proprietor or an impatient customer called out her name, Beatrice; then other customers would raise their heads briefly, a few seconds, as if to behold the bearer of such a beautiful name, but not finding anybody there, they would resume their drinking, their ribald jokes, their laughter and play with the other serving girls. She was like a wounded bird in flight: a forced landing now and then but nevertheless wobbling from place to place so that she would variously be found in Alaska, Paradise, The Modern, Thome and other beer-halls all over Limuru. Sometimes it was because an irate proprietor found she was not attracting enough customers; he would sack her without notice and without a salary. She would wobble to the next bar. But sometimes she was simply tired of nesting in one place, a daily witness of familiar scenes; girls even more decidedly ugly than she were fought over by numerous claimants at closing hours. What do they have that I don't have? She would ask herself, depressed. She longed for a bar-kingdom where she would be at least one of the rulers, where petitioners would bring their gifts of beer, frustrated smiles and often curses that hid more lust and love than hate.

She left Limuru town proper and tried the mushrooming townlets around. She worked at Ngarariga, Kamiritho, Rironi and even Tiekunu and everywhere the story was the same. Oh, yes, occasionally she would get a client; but none cared for her as she would have liked, none really wanted her enough to fight over her. She was always a hard-up customer's last resort. No make-believe even, not for her that sweet pretence that men indulged in after their fifth bottle of Tusker. The following night or during a pay-day, the same client would pretend not to know her; he would be trying his money-power over girls who already had more than a fair share of admirers.

She resented this. She saw in every girl a rival and adopted a sullen attitude. Nyagūthiï especially was the thorn that always pricked her wounded flesh. Nyagūthiï, arrogant and aloof, but men always in her courtyard; Nyagūthiï, fighting with men, and to her they would bring propitiating gifts which she accepted as of right. Nyagūthiï could look bored, impatient, or downright contemptuous and still men would cling to her as if they enjoyed being whipped with biting words, curled lips and the indifferent eyes of a free woman. Nyagūthiï was also a bird in flight, never really able to settle in one place, but in her case it was because she hungered for change and excitement: new faces and new territories for her conquest. Beatrice resented her very shadow. She saw in her the girl she would have liked to be, a girl who was both totally immersed in and yet completely above the underworld of bar violence and sex. Wherever Beatrice went the long shadow of Nyagūthiï would sooner or later follow her.

She fled Limuru for Ilmorog in Chiri District. Ilmorog had once been a ghost village, but had been resurrected to life by that legendary woman, Nyang'endo, to whom every pop group had paid their tribute. It was of her that the young dancing Muthuu and Muchun g' wa sang:

When I left Nairobi for Ilmorog
Never did I know
I would bear this wonder-child mine
Nyang'endo.

As a result, Ilmorog was always seen as a town of hope where the weary and the down-trodden would find their rest and fresh water. But again Nyagũthiĩ followed her.

She found that Ilmorog, despite the legend, despite the songs and dances, was not different from Limuru. She tried various tricks. Clothes? But even here she never earned enough to buy herself glittering robes. What was seventy-five shillings a month without house allowance, *posho*, without salaried boy-friends? By that time, Ambi had reached Ilmorog, and Beatrice thought that this would be the answer. Had she not, in Limuru, seen girls blacker than herself transformed overnight from ugly sins into white stars by a touch of skin-lightening creams? And men would ogle them, would even talk with exaggerated pride of their newborn girl friends. Men were strange creatures, Beatrice thought in moments of searching analysis. They talked heatedly against Ambi, Butone, Firesnow, Moonsnow, wigs, straightened hair; but they always went for a girl with an Ambi-lightened skin and head covered with a wig made in imitation of European or Indian hair. Beatrice never tried to find the root cause of this black self-hatred, she simply accepted the contradiction and applied herself to Ambi with a vengeance. She had to rub out her black shame. But even Ambi she could not afford in abundance; she could only apply it to her face and to her arms so that her legs and her neck retained their blackness. Besides there were parts of her face she could not readily reach – behind the ears and above the eyelashes, for instance – and these were a constant source of shame and irritation to her Ambi-self.

She would always remember this Ambi period as one of her deepest humiliation before her later minutes of glory. She worked in Ilmorog Starlight Bar and Lodging. Nyagũthiĩ, with her bangled hands, her huge earrings, served behind the counter. The owner was a good Christian soul who regularly went to church and paid all his dues to *Harambee* projects. Pot-belly. Grey hairs. Soft-spoken. A respectable family man, well known in Ilmorog. Hardworking even, for he would not leave the bar until the closing hours, or more precisely, until Nyagũthiĩ left. He had no eyes for any other girl; he hung around her, and surreptitiously brought her gifts of clothes without receiving gratitude in kind. Only the promise. Only the hope for to-morrow. Other girls he gave eighty shillings a month. Nyagũthiĩ had a room to herself. Nyagũthiĩ woke up whenever she liked to take the stock. But Beatrice and the other girls had to wake up at five or so, make tea for the lodgers, clean up the bar and wash dishes and glasses. Then they would hang around the bar in shifts until two o'clock when they would go for a small break. At five o'clock, they had to be in again, ready for customers whom they would now serve with frothy beers and smiles until twelve o'clock or for as long as there were customers thirsty for more Tuskers and Pilsners. What often galled Beatrice, although in her case it did not matter one way or another, was the owner's insistence that the girls should sleep in Starlight. They would otherwise be late for work, he said. But what he really wanted was for the girls to use their bodies to attract more lodgers in Starlight. Most of the girls, led by Nyagũthiĩ, defied the rule and bribed the watchman to let them out and in. They wanted to meet their regular or one-night boy-friends in places where they would be free and where they would be treated as not just barmaids. Beatrice always slept in. Her occasional one-night patrons wanted to spend the minimum. Came a night when the owner, refused by Nyagũthiĩ, approached her. He started by finding fault with her work; he called her names, then as sud-denly he started praising her, although in a grudging almost contemptuous manner. He grabbed her, struggled with her, pot-belly, grey hairs, and everything. Beatrice felt an unusual revulsion for the man. She could not, she would not bring her-self to accept that which had so recently been cast aside by Nyagũthiĩ. My God, she wept inside, what does Nyagũthiĩ have that I don't have? The man now humiliated himself before her. He implored. He promised her gifts. But she would not yield. That night she too defied the rule. She jumped through a window; she sought a bed in another bar and only came back at six. The proprietor called her in front of all the others and dismissed her. But Beatrice was rather surprised at herself.

She stayed a month without a job. She lived from room to room at the capricious mercy of the other girls. She did not have the heart to leave Ilmorog and start all over again in a new town. The wound hurt. She was tired of wandering. She stopped using Ambi. No money. She looked at herself in the mirror. She had so aged, hardly a year after she had fallen from grace. Why then was she scrupulous, she would ask herself. But somehow she had a horror of soliciting lovers or directly barter-ing her body for hard cash. What she wanted was decent work and a man or several men who cared for her. Perhaps she took that need for a man, for a home and for a child with her to bed. Perhaps it was this genuine need that scared off men who wanted other things from barmaids. She wept late at nights and remem-bered home. At such moments, her mother's village in Nyeri seemed the sweetest place on God's earth. She would invest the life of her peasant mother and father with romantic illusions of immeasurable peace and harmony. She longed to go back home to see them. But how could she go back with empty hands? In any case the place was now a distant landscape in the memory. Her life was here in the bar among this crowd of lost strangers. Fallen from grace, fallen from grace. She was part of a generation which would never again be one with the soil, the crops, the wind and the moon. Not for them that whispering in dark hedges, not for her that dance and love-making under the glare of the moon, with the hills of TumuTumu rising to touch the sky. She remembered that girl from her home village who, despite a life of apparent glamour being the kept mistress of one rich man after another in Limuru, had gassed herself to death. This generation was not awed by the mystery of death, just as it was callous to the mystery of life; for how many unmarried mothers had thrown their babies into latrines rather than lose that glamour? The girl's death became the subject of jokes. She had gone metric – without pains, they said. Thereafter, for a week, Beatrice thought of going metric. But she could not bring herself to do it.

She wanted love; she wanted life.

A new bar was opened in Ilmorog. Treetop Bar, Lodging and Restaurant. Why Treetop, Beatrice could not understand unless because it was a storied building: tea-shop on the ground floor and beer-shop in a room at the top. The rest were rooms for five-minute or one-night lodgers. The owner was a retired civil servant but one who still played at politics. He was enormously wealthy with business sites and enterprises in every major town in Kenya. Big shots from all over the country came to his bar. Big men in Mercedez. Big men in their Bentleys. Big men in their Jaguars and Daimlers. Big men with uniformed chauffeurs drowsing with boredom in cars waiting outside. There were others not so big who came to pay respects to the great. They talked politics mostly. And about their work. Gossip was rife. Didn't you know? Indeed so and so has been promoted. Really? And so and so has been sacked. Embezzlement of public funds. So foolish you know. Not clever about it at all. They argued, they quarrelled, sometimes they fought it out with fists, especially during the elections campaign. The only point on which they were all agreed was that the Luo community was the root cause of all the trouble in Kenya; that intellectuals and University students were living in an ivory tower of privilege and arrogance; that Kiambu had more than a lion's share of developments; that men from Nyeri and Muranga had acquired all the big business in Nairobi and were even encroaching on Chiri District; that African workers, especially those on the farms, were lazy and jealous of 'us' who had sweated ourselves to sudden prosperity. Otherwise each would hymn his own praises or return compliments. Occasionally in moments of drunken ebullience and self-praise, one would order two rounds of beer for each man present in the bar. Even the poor from

Ilmorog would come to Treetop to dine at the gates of the
nouveaux riches.

Here Beatrice got a job as a sweeper and bedmaker. Here for
a few weeks she felt closer to greatness. Now she made beds for
men she had previously known as names. She watched how even
the poor tried to drink and act big in front of the big. But soon
fate caught up with her. Girls flocked to Treetop from other
bars. Girls she had known at Limuru, girls she had known at
Ilmorog. And most had attached themselves to one or several
big men, often playing a hide-and-not-to-be-found game with
their numerous lovers. And Nyagūthiī was there behind the
counter, with the eyes of the rich and the poor fixed on her. And
she, with her big eyes, bangled hands and earrings maintained
the same air of bored indifference. Beatrice as a sweeper and bedmaker became even more invisible. Girls who had fallen into
good fortune looked down upon her.

She fought life with dreams. In between putting clean sheets
on beds that had just witnessed a five-minute struggle that ended
in a half-strangled cry and a pool, she would stand by the
window and watch the cars and the chauffeurs, so that soon she
knew all the owners by the number plates of their cars and the
uniforms of their chauffeurs. She dreamt of lovers who would
come for her in sleek Mercedes sports cars made for two. She
saw herself linking hands with such a lover, walking in the streets
of Nairobi and Mombasa, tapping the ground with high heels,
quick, quick short steps. And suddenly she would stop in front of
a display glass window, exclaiming at the same time; Oh darling,
won't you buy me those . . . ? Those what, he would ask, affecting anger. Those stockings, darling. It was as an owner of several
stockings, ladderless and holeless, that she thought of her well-
being. Never again would she mend torn things. Never, never,
never. Do you understand? Never. She was next the proud owner
of different coloured wigs, blonde wigs, brunette wigs, Redhead
wigs, Afro wigs, wigs, wigs, all the wigs in the world. Only then
would the whole earth sing hallelujah to the one Beatrice. At

such moments, she would feel exalted, lifted out of her murky self, no longer a floor sweeper and bedmaker for a five-minute instant love, but Beatrice, descendant of Wangu Makeri who made men tremble with desire at her naked body bathed in moonlight, daughter of Nyang'endo, the founder of modern Ilmorog, of whom they often sang that she had worked several lovers into impotence.

Then she noticed him and he was the opposite of the lover of her dreams. He came one Saturday afternoon driving a big five-ton lorry. He carefully parked it beside the Benzes, the Jaguars and the Daimlers, not as a lorry, but as one of those sleek cream-bodied frames, so proud of it he seemed to be. He dressed in a baggy grey suit over which he wore a heavy khaki military overcoat. He removed the overcoat, folded it with care, and put it in the front seat. He locked all the doors, dusted himself a little, then walked round the lorry as if inspecting it for damage. A few steps before he entered Treetop, he turned round for a final glance at his lorry dwarfing the other things. At Treetops he sat in a corner and, with a rather loud defiant voice, ordered a Kenya one. He drank it with relish, looking around at the same time for a face he might recognize. He indeed did recognize one of the big ones and he immediately ordered for him a quarter bottle of Vat 69. This was accepted with a bare nod of the head and a patronizing smile; but when he tried to follow his generosity with a conversation, he was firmly ignored. He froze, sank into his Muratina. But only for a time. He tried again: he was met with frowning faces. More pathetic were his attempts to join in jokes; he would laugh rather too loudly, which would make the big ones stop, leaving him in the air alone. Later in the evening he stood up, counted several crisp hundred shilling notes and handed them to Nyagũthiĩ behind the counter ostensibly for safekeeping. People whispered; murmured; a few laughed, rather derisively, though they were rather impressed. But this act did not win him immediate recognition. He staggered towards room no. 7 which he had hired. Beatrice brought him the keys. He glanced at her, briefly, then lost all interest.

Thereafter he came every Saturday. At five when most of the big shots were already seated. He repeated the same ritual, except the money act, and always met with defeat. He nearly always sat in the same corner and always rented room 7. Beatrice grew to anticipate his visits and, without being conscious of it, kept the room ready for him. Often after he had been badly humiliated by the big company, he would detain Beatrice and talk to her, or rather he talked to himself in her presence. For him, it had been a life of struggles. He had never been to school although getting an education had been his ambition. He never had a chance. His father was a squatter in the European settled area in the Rift Valley. That meant a lot in those colonial days. It meant among other things a man and his children were doomed to a future of sweat and toil for the white devils and their children. He had joined the freedom struggle and like the others had been sent to detention. He came from detention the same as his mother had brought him to this world. Nothing. With independence he found he did not possess the kind of education which would have placed him in one of the vacancies at the top. He started as a charcoal burner, then a butcher, gradually working his own way to become a big transporter of vegetables and potatoes from the Rift Valley and Chiri districts to Nairobi. He was proud of his achievement. But he resented that others, who had climbed to their present wealth through loans and a subsidized education, would not recognize his like. He would rumble on like this, dwelling on education he would never have, and talking of better chances for his children. Then he would carefully count the money, put it under the pillow, and then dismiss Beatrice. Occasionally he would buy her a beer but he was clearly suspicious of women whom he saw as money-eaters of men. He had not yet married.

One night he slept with her. In the morning he scratched for a twenty shilling note and gave it to her. She accepted the money with an odd feeling of guilt. He did this for several weeks. She did not mind the money. It was useful. But he paid for her body as he would pay for a bag of potatoes or a sack of cabbages. With the one pound, he had paid for her services as a listener, a vessel of his complaints against those above, and as a one-night receptacle of his man's burden. She was becoming bored with his ego, with his stories that never varied in content, but somehow, in him, deep inside, she felt that something had been there, a fire, a seed, a flower which was being smothered. In him she saw a fellow victim and looked forward to his visits. She too longed to talk to someone. She too longed to confide in a human being who would understand.

And she did it one Saturday night, suddenly interrupting the story of his difficult climb to the top. She did not know why she did it. Maybe it was the rain outside. It was softly drumming the corrugated iron sheets, bringing with the drumming a warm and drowsy indifference. He would listen. He had to listen. She came from Karatina in Nyeri. Her two brothers had been gunned down by the British soldiers. Another one had died in detention. She was, so to speak, an only child. Her parents were poor. But they worked hard on their bare strip of land and managed to pay her fees in primary school. For the first six years she had worked hard. In the seventh year, she must have relaxed a little. She did not pass with a good grade. Of course she knew many with similar grades who had been called to good government secondary schools. She knew a few others with lesser grades who had gone to very top schools on the strength of their connections. But she was not called to any high school with reasonable fees. Her parents could not afford fees in a Harambee school. And she would not hear of repeating standard seven. She stayed at home with her parents. Occasionally she would help them in the shamba and with house chores. But imagine: for the past six years she had led a life with a different rhythm from that of her parents. Life in the village was dull. She would often go to Karatina and to Nyeri in search of work. In every office, they would ask her the same questions: what work do you want? What do you know?

Can you type? Can you take shorthand? She was desperate. It was in Nyeri, drinking Fanta in a shop, tears in her eyes, that she met a young man in a dark suit and sun-glasses. He saw her plight and talked to her. He came from Nairobi. Looking for work? That's easy; in a big city there would be no difficulty with jobs. He would certainly help. Transport? He had a car – a cream-white Peugeot. Heaven. It was a beautiful ride, with the promise of dawn. Nairobi. He drove her to Terrace Bar. They drank beer and talked about Nairobi. Through the window she could see the neon-lit city and knew that here was hope. That night she gave herself to him, with the promise of dawn making her feel light and gay. She had a very deep sleep. When she woke in the morning, the man in the cream-white Peugeot was not there. She never saw him again. That's how she had started the life of a barmaid. And for one and half years now she had not been once to see her parents. Beatrice started weeping. Huge sobs of self-pity. Her humiliation and constant flight were fresh in her mind. She had never been able to take to bar culture, she always thought that something better would come her way. But she was trapped, it was the only life she now knew, although she had never really learnt all its laws and norms. Again she heaved out and in, tears tossing out with every sob. Then suddenly she froze. Her sobbing was arrested in the air. The man had long covered himself. His snores were huge and unmistakable.

She felt a strange hollowness. Then a bile of bitterness spilt inside her. She wanted to cry at her new failure. She had met several men who had treated her cruelly, who had laughed at her scruples, at what they thought was an ill-disguised attempt at innocence. She had accepted. But not this, Lord, not this. Was this man not a fellow victim? Had he not, Saturday after Saturday, unburdened himself to her? He had paid for her human services; he had paid away his responsibility with his bottle of Tuskers and hard cash in the morning. Her innermost turmoil had been his lullaby. And suddenly something in her snapped.

All the anger of a year and a half, all the bitterness against her humiliation were now directed at this man.

What she did later had the mechanical precision of an experienced hand.

She touched his eyes. He was sound asleep. She raised his head. She let it fall. Her tearless eyes were now cold and set. She removed the pillow from under him. She rummaged through it. She took out his money. She counted five crisp pink notes. She put the money inside her brassiere.

She went out of room no. 7. Outside it was still raining. She did not want to go to her usual place. She could not now stand the tiny cupboard room or the superior chatter of her room-mate. She walked through mud and rain. She found herself walking towards Nyagūthii's room. She knocked at the door. At first she had no response. Then she heard Nyagūthii's sleepy voice above the drumming rain.

'Who is that?'

'It is me. Please open.'

'Who?'

'Beatrice.'

'At this hour of the night?'

'Please.'

Lights were put on. Bolts unfastened. The door opened. Beatrice stepped inside. She and Nyagūthii stood there face to face. Nyagūthii was in a see-through nightdress: on her shoulders she had a green pullover.

'Beatrice, is there anything wrong?' She at last asked, a note of concern in her voice.

'Can I rest here for a while? I am tired. And I want to talk to you.' Beatrice's voice carried assurance and power.

'But what has happened?'

'I only want to ask you a question, Nyagūthii.'

They were still standing. Then, without a word, they both sat on the bed.

'Why did you leave home, Nyagūthii?' Beatrice asked.

Another silent moment. Nyagūthiī seemed to be thinking about the question. Beatrice waited. Nyagūthiī's voice when at last it came was slightly tremulous, unsteady.

'It is a long story, Beatrice. My father and mother were fairly wealthy. They were also good Christians. We lived under regulations. You must never walk with the heathen. You must not attend their pagan customs — dances and circumcision rites, for instance. There were rules about what, how and when to eat. You must even walk like a Christian lady. You must never be seen with boys. Rules, rules all the way. One day instead of returning home from school, I and another girl from a similar home ran away to Eastleigh. I have never been home once this last four years. That's all.'

Another silence. Then they looked at one another in mutual recognition.

'One more question, Nyagūthiī. You need not answer it. But I have always thought that you hated me, you despised me.'

'No, no, Beatrice, I have never hated you. I have never hated anybody. It is just that nothing interests me. Even men do not move me now. Yet I want, I need instant excitement. I need the attention of those false flattering eyes to make me feel myself, myself. But you, you seemed above all this — somehow you had something inside you that I did not have.'

Beatrice tried to hold her tears with difficulty.

Early the next day, she boarded a bus bound for Nairobi. She walked down Bazaar street looking at the shops. Then down Government Road, right into Kenyatta Avenue, and Kimathi street. She went into a shop near Hussein Suleman's street and bought several stockings. She put on a pair. She next bought herself a new dress. Again she changed into it. In a Bata Shoe-shop, she bought high heeled shoes, put them on and discarded her old flat ones. On to an Akamba kiosk, and she fitted herself with earrings. She went to a mirror and looked at her new self. Suddenly she felt enormous hunger as if she had been hungry all her life. She hesitated in front of Moti Mahal. Then she walked on, eventually entering Fransae. There was a glint in her eyes that made men's eyes turn to her. This thrilled her. She chose a table in a corner and ordered Indian curry. A man left his table and joined her. She looked at him. Her eyes were merry. He was dressed in a dark suit and his eyes spoke of lust. He bought her a drink. He tried to engage her in conversation. But she ate in silence. He put his hand under the table and felt her knees. She let him do it. The hand went up and up her thigh. Then suddenly she left her unfinished food and her untouched drink and walked out. She felt good. He followed her. She knew this without once turning her eyes. He walked beside her for a few yards. She smiled at herself but did not look at him. He lost his confidence. She left him standing sheepishly looking at a glass window outside Gino's. In the bus back to Ilmorog, men gave her seats. She accepted this as of right. At Treetops bar she went straight to the counter. The usual crowd of big men was there. Their conversations stopped for a few seconds at her entry. Their lascivious eyes were turned to her. The girls stared at her. Even Nyagũthiĩ could not maintain her bored indifference. Beatrice bought them drinks. The manager came to her, rather unsure. He tried a conversation. Why had she left work? Where had she been? Would she like to work in the bar, helping Nyagũthiĩ behind the counter? Now and then? A barmaid brought her a note. A certain big shot wanted to know if she would join their table. More notes came from different big quarters with the one question; would she be free tonight? A trip to Nairobi even. She did not leave her place at the counter. But she accepted their drinks as of right. She felt a new power, confidence even.

She took out a shilling, put it in the slot and the juke box boomed with the voice of Robinson Mwangi singing Hũnyũ wa Mashambani. He sang of those despised girls who worked on farms and contrasted them with urban girls. Then she played a Kamaru and a D.K. Men wanted to dance with her. She ignored them, but enjoyed their flutter around her. She twisted her hips to the sound of yet another D.K. Her body was free. She was free. She sucked in the excitement and tension in the air.

Then suddenly at around six, the man with the five-ton Lorry stormed into the bar. This time he had on his military overcoat. Behind him was a policeman. He looked around. Everybody's eyes were raised to him. But Beatrice went on swaying her hips. At first he could not recognize Beatrice in the girl celebrating her few minutes of glory by the juke box. Then he shouted in triumph. 'That is the girl! Thief! Thief!'

People melted back to their seats. The policeman went and handcuffed her. She did not resist. Only at the door she turned her head and spat. Then she went out followed by the policeman.

In the bar the stunned silence broke into hilarious laughter when someone made a joke about sweetened robbery without violence. They discussed her. Some said she should have been beaten. Others talked contemptuously about 'these bar girls.' Yet others talked with a concern noticeable in unbelieving shakes of their heads about the rising rate of crime. Shouldn't the Hanging Bill be extended to all thefts of property? And without anybody being aware of it the man with the five-ton lorry had become a hero. They now surrounded him with questions and demanded the whole story. Some even bought him drinks. More remarkable, they listened, their attentive silence punctuated by appreciative laughter. The averted threat to property had temporarily knit them into one family. And the man, accepted for the first time, told the story with relish.

But behind the counter Nyagūthii wept.

WEDDING AT THE CROSS

Everyone said of them: what a nice family; he, the successful timber merchant; and she, the obedient wife who did her duty to God, husband and family. Wariuki and his wife Miriamu were a shining example of what cooperation between man and wife united in love and devotion could achieve: he tall, correct, even a little stiff, but wealthy; she, small, quiet, unobtrusive, a diminishing shadow beside her giant of a husband.

He had married her when he was without a cent buried anywhere, not even for the rainiest day, for he was then only a milk clerk in a settler farm earning thirty shillings a month—a fortune in those days, true, but drinking most of it by the first of the next month. He was young; he did not care; dreams of material possessions and power little troubled him. Of course he joined the other workers in collective protests and demands, he would even compose letters for them; from one or two farms he had been dismissed as a dangerous and subversive character. But his heart was really elsewhere, in his favourite sports and acts. He would proudly ride his Raleigh Bicycle around, whistling certain lines from old records remembered, yodelling in imitation of Jim Rogers, and occasionally demonstrating his skill on the machine to an enthusiastic audience in Molo township. He would stand on the bicycle balancing with the left leg, arms stretched about to fly, or he would simply pedal backwards to the delight of many children. It was an old machine, but decorated in loud colours of red, green and blue with several Wariuki home-manufactured headlamps and reflectors and with a warning scrawled on a signboard mounted at the back seat: Overtake Me, Graveyard Ahead. From a conjurer on a bicycle, he would move to other roles. See the actor now mimicking his white bosses, satirizing their way of

talking and walking and also their mannerisms and attitudes to
black workers. Even those Africans who sought favours from
the whites were not spared. He would vary his acts with dancing,
good dancer too, and his mwomboko steps, with the left trouser
leg deliberately split along the seam to an inch above the knee,
always attracted approving eyes and sighs from maids in the
crowd.

That's how he first captured Miriamu's heart.

On every Sunday afternoon she would seize any opportunity
to go to the shopping square where she would eagerly join the
host of worshippers. Her heart would then rise and fall with his
triumphs and narrow escapes, or simply pound in rhythm with
his dancing hips. Miriamu's family was miles better off than most
squatters in the Rift Valley. Her father, Douglas Jones, owned
several groceries and tea-rooms around the town. A God-fearing
couple he and his wife were: they went to church on Sundays,
they said their prayers first thing in the morning, last thing in
the evening and of course before every meal. They were looked
on with favour by the white farmers around; the District Officer
would often stop by for a casual greeting. Theirs then was a
good Christian home and hence they objected to their daughter
marrying into sin, misery and poverty: what could she possibly
see in that Murebi, Murebi bii-u? They told her not to attend those
heathen Sunday scenes of idleness and idol worship. But
Miriamu had an independent spirit, though it had since childhood
been schooled into inactivity by Sunday sermons – thou shalt
obey thy father and mother and those that rule over us – and a
proper upbringing with rules straight out of the Rt. Reverend
Clive Schomberg's classic: *British Manners for Africans*. Now
Wariuki with his Raleigh bicycle, his milkman's tunes, his
baggy trousers and dance which gave freedom to the body, was
the light that beckoned her from the sterile world of Douglas
Jones to a neon-lit city in a far horizon. Part of her was suspicious
of the heavy glow, she was even slightly revolted by his dirt and
patched up trousers, but she followed him, and was surprised at

her firmness. Douglas Jones relented a little: he loved his daughter and only desired the best for her. He did not want her to marry one of those useless half-educated upstarts, who disturbed the ordered life, peace and prosperity on European farms. Such men, as the Bwana District Officer often told him, would only end in jails: they were motivated by greed and wanted to cheat the simple-hearted and illiterate workers about the evils of white settlers and missionaries. Wariuki looked the dangerous type in every way.

He summoned Wariuki, 'Our would-be-son-in-law', to his presence. He wanted to find the young man's true weight in silver and gold. And Wariuki, with knees weakened a little, for he, like most workers, was a little awed by men of that Christian and propertied class, carefully mended his left trouser leg, combed and brushed his hair and went there. They made him stand at the door, without offering him a chair, and surveyed him up and down. Wariuki, bewildered, looked alternately to Miriamu and to the wall for possible deliverance. And then when he finally got a chair, he would not look at the parents and the dignitaries invited to sit in judgement but fixed his eyes to the wall. But he was aware of their naked gaze and condemnation. Douglas Jones, though, was a model of Christian graciousness: tea for our – well – our son – well – this young man here. What work? Milk clerk? Ahh, well, well – no man was born with wealth – wealth was in the limbs you know and you, you are so young – salary? Thirty shillings a month? Well, well, others had climbed up from worse and deeper pits: true wealth came from the Lord on high, you know. And Wariuki was truly grateful for these words and even dared a glance and a smile at old Douglas Jones. What he saw in those eyes made him quickly turn to the wall and wait for the execution. The manner of the execution was not rough: but the cold steel cut deep and clean. Why did Wariuki want to marry when he was so young? Well, well, as you like – the youth today – so different from our time. And who 'are we' to tell what youth ought to do? We do not object to the

wedding: but we as Christians have a responsibility. I say it again:
we do not object to this union. But it must take place at the cross.
A church wedding, Wariuki, costs money. Maintaining a wife
also costs money. Is that not so? You nod your head? Good. It is
nice to see a young man with sense these days. All that I now
want, and that is why I have called in my counsellor friends, is to
see your savings account. Young man, can you show these
elders your post office book?

Wariuki was crushed. He now looked at the bemused eyes of
the elders present. He then fixed them on Miriamu's mother, as if
in appeal. Only he was not seeing her. Away from the teats and
rich udder of the cows, away from his bicycle and the crowd of
rich admirers, away from the anonymous security of bars and
tea-shops, he did not know how to act. He was a hunted animal,
now cornered: and the hunters, panting with anticipation, were
enjoying every moment of that kill. A buzz in his head, a blurring
vision, and he heard the still gracious voice of Douglas Jones
trailing into something about not signing his daughter to a life of
misery and drudgery. Desperately Wariuki looked to the door
and to the open space.

Escape at last: and he breathed with relief. Although he was
trembling a little, he was glad to be in a familiar world, his own
world. But he looked at it slightly differently, almost as if he
had been wounded and could not any more enjoy what he saw.
Miriamu followed him there: for a moment he felt a temporary
victory over Douglas Jones. They ran away and he got a job
with Ciana Timber Merchants in Ilmorog forest. The two lived in
a shack of a room to which he escaped from the daily curses of his
Indian employers. Wariuki learnt how to endure the insults. He
sang with the movement of the saw: kneeling down under the
log, the other man standing on it, he would make up words and
stories about the log and the forest, sometimes ending on a tragic
note when he came to the fatal marriage between the saw and the
forest. This somehow would lighten his heart so that he did not
mind the falling saw-dust. Came his turn to stand on top of the

log and he would experience a malicious power as he sawed
through it, gingerly walking backwards step by step and now
singing of Demi na Mathathi who, long ago, cleared woods and
forests more dense than Ilmorog.

And Miriamu the erstwhile daughter of Douglas Jones would
hear his voice rising above the whispering or uproarious wind
and her heart rose and fell with it. This, this, dear Lord, was so
different from the mournful church hymns of her father's
compound, so, so, different and she felt good inside. On Satur-
days and Sundays he took her to dances in the wood. On their
way home from the dances and the songs, they would look for a
suitable spot on the grass and make love. For Miriamu these
were nights of happiness and wonder as the thorny pine leaves
painfully but pleasantly pricked her buttocks even as she moaned
under him, calling out to her mother and imaginary sisters for
help when he plunged into her.

And Wariuki too was happy. It always seemed to him a miracle
that he, a boy from the streets and without a father (he had died
while carrying guns and food for the British in their expeditions
against the Germans in Tanganyika in the first European
World War), had secured the affections of a girl from that class.
But he was never the old Wariuki. Often he would go over his
life beginning with his work picking pyrethrum flowers for
others under a scorching sun or icy cold winds in Limuru, to his
recent job as a milk clerk in Molo: his reminiscences would
abruptly end with that interview with Douglas Jones and his
counsellors. He would never forget that interview: he was never
to forget the cackling throaty laughter as Douglas Jones and his
friends tried to diminish his manhood and selfworth in front of
Miriamu and her mother.

Never. He would show them. He would yet laugh in their
faces.

But soon a restless note crept into his singing: bitterness of an
unfulfilled hope and promise. His voice became rugged like the
voice-teeth of the saw and he tore through the air with the same

greedy malice. He gave up his job with the Ciana Merchants and took Miriamu all the way to Limuru. He dumped Miriamu with his aged mother and he disappeared from their lives. They heard of him in Nairobi, Mombasa, Nakuru, Kisumu and even Kampala. Rumours reached them: that he was in prison, that he had even married a Muganda girl. Miriamu waited: she remembered her moments of pained pleasure under Ilmorog woods, ferns and grass and endured the empty bed and the bite of Limuru cold in June and July. Her parents had disowned her and anyway she would not want to go back. The seedling he had planted in her warmed her. Eventually the child arrived and this together with the simple friendship of her mother-in-law consoled her. Came more rumours: whitemen were gathering arms for a war amongst themselves, and black men, sons of the soil, were being drafted to aid in the slaughter. Could this be true? Then Wariuki returned from his travels and she noticed the change in her man. He was now of few words: where was the singing and the whistling of old tunes remembered? He stayed a week. Then he said: I am going to war. Miriamu could not understand: why this change? Why this wanderlust? But she waited and worked on the land.

Wariuki had the one obsession: to erase the memory of that interview, to lay for ever the ghost of those contemptuous eyes. He fought in Egypt, Palestine, Burma and in Madagascar. He did not think much about the war, he did not question what it meant for black people, he just wanted it to end quickly so that he might resume his quest. Why, he might even go home with a little loot from the war. This would give him the start in life he had looked for, without success, in towns all over Colonial Kenya. A lucrative job even: the British had promised them jobs and money-rewards once the wicked Germans were routed. After the war he was back in Limuru, a little emaciated in body but hardened in resolve.

For a few weeks after his return, Miriamu detected a little flicker of the old fires and held him close to herself. He made a few jokes about the war, and sang a few soldiers' songs to his

son. He made love to her and another seed was planted. He
again tried to get a job. He heard of a workers' strike in a
Limuru shoe factory. All the workers were summarily dismissed.
Wariuki and others flooded the gates to offer their sweat for
silver. The striking workers tried to picket the new hands, whom
they branded traitors to the cause, but helmeted police were
called to the scene, baton charged the old workers away from the
fenced compound and escorted the new ones into the factory.
But Wariuki was not among them. Was he born into bad luck?
He was back in the streets of Nairobi joining the crowd of the
unemployed recently returned from the War. No jobs no
money-rewards: the 'good' British and the 'wicked' Germans
were shaking hands with smiles. But questions as to why black
people were not employed did not trouble him: when young men
gathered in Pumwani, Kariokor, Shauri Moyo and other places
to ask questions he did not join them: they reminded him of his
old association and flirtation with farm workers before the war:
those efforts had come to nought: even these ones would come to
nought: he was in any case ashamed of that past: he thought that
if he had been less of a loafer and more enterprising he would
never have been so humiliated in front of Miriamu and her
mother. The young men's talk of processions, petitions and pis-
tols, their talk of gunning the whites out of the country, seemed
too remote from his ambition and quest. He had to strike out on
his own for moneyland. On arrival, he would turn round and con-
front old Douglas Jones and contemptuously flaunt success before
his face. With the years the memory of that humiliation in the
hands of the rich became so sharp and fresh that it often hurt him
into sleepless nights. He did not think of the whites and the
Indians as the real owners of property, commerce and land. He
only saw the picture of Douglas Jones in his grey woollen suit, his
waistcoat, his hat and his walking stick of a folded umbrella.
What was the secret of that man's success? What? What? He
attempted odd jobs here and there: he even tried his hand at
trading in the hawk market at Bahati. He would buy pencils and

handkerchiefs from the Indian Bazaar and sell them at a retail price that ensured him a bit of profit. Was this his true vocation?

But before he could find an answer to his question, the Mau Mau war of national liberation broke out. A lot of workers, employed and unemployed, were swept off the streets of Nairobi into concentration camps. Somehow he escaped the net and was once again back in Limuru. He was angry. Not with the whites, not with the Indians, all of whom he saw as permanent features of the land like the mountains and the valleys, but with his own people. Why should they upset the peace? Why should they upset the stability just when he had started gathering a few cents from his trade? He now believed, albeit without much conviction, the lies told by the British about imminent prosperity and widening opportunities for blacks. For about a year he remained aloof from the turmoil around: he was only committed to his one consuming passion. Then he drifted into the hands of the colonial regime and cooperated. This way he avoided concentration camps and the forest. Soon his choice of sides started bearing fruit: he was excited about the prospects for its ripening. While other people's strips of land were being taken by the colonialists, his piece, although small, was left intact. In fact, during land consolidation forced on women and old men while their husbands and sons were decaying in detention or resisting in the forest, he, along with other active collaborators, secured additional land. Wariuki was not a cruel man: he just wanted this nightmare over so that he might resume his trade. For even in the midst of battle the image of D. Jones never really left him: the humiliation ached: he nursed it like one nurses a toothache with one's tongue, and felt that a day would come when he would stand up to that image.

Jomo Kenyatta returned home from Maralal. Wariuki was a little frightened, his spirits were dampened: what would happen to his kind at the gathering of the braves to celebrate victory? Alas, where were the Whites he had thought of as permanent features of the landscape? But with independence approaching, Wariuki had his first real reward: the retreating colonialists gave him a loan: he bought a motor-propelled saw and set up as a Timber Merchant.

For a time after Independence, Wariuki feared for his life and business as the sons of the soil streamed back from detention camps and from the forests: he expected a retribution, but people were tired. They had no room in their hearts for vengeance at the victorious end of a just struggle. So Wariuki prospered undisturbed: he had, after all, a fair start over those who had really fought for Uhuru.

He joined the Church in gratitude. The Lord had spared him: he dragged Miriamu into it, and together they became exemplary Church-goers.

But Miriamu prayed a different prayer, she wanted her man back. Her two sons were struggling their way through Siriana Secondary School. For this she thanked the Lord. But she still wanted her real Wariuki back. During the Emergency she had often cautioned him against excessive cruelty. It pained her that his singing, his dancing and his easy laughter had ended. His eyes were hard and set and this frightened her.

Now in Church he started singing again. Not the tunes that had once captured her soul, but the mournful hymns she knew so well; how sweet the name of Jesus sounds in a believer's ears. He became a pillar of the Church Choir. He often beat the drum which, after Independence, had been introduced into the church as a concession to African culture. He attended classes in baptism and great was the day he cast away Wariuki and became Dodge W. Livingstone, Jr. Thereafter he sat in the front bench. As his business improved, he gradually worked his way to the holy aisle. A new Church elder.

Other things brightened. His parents-in-law still lived in Molo, though their fortunes had declined. They had not yet forgiven him. But with his eminence, they sent out feelers: would their daughter pay them a visit? Miriamu would not hear of it. But Dodge W. Livingstone was furious: where was her Christian forgiveness? He was insistent. She gave in. He was glad. But that gesture, by itself, could not erase the memory of his humiliation. His vengeance would still come.

Though his base was at Limuru, he travelled to various parts of the country. So he got to know news concerning his line of business. It was the year of the Asian exodus. Ciana Merchants were not Kenya Citizens. Their licence would be withdrawn. They quickly offered Livingstone partnership on a fifty-fifty share basis. Praise the Lord and raise high his name. Truly God never ate Ugali. Within a year he had accumulated enough to qualify for a loan to buy one of the huge farms in Limuru previously owned by whites. He was now a big timber merchant: they made him a senior elder of the church.

Miriamu still waited for her Wariuki in vain. But she was a model wife. People praised her Christian and wifely meekness. She was devout in her own way and prayed to the Lord to rescue her from the dreams of the past. She never put on airs. She even refused to wear shoes. Every morning, she would wake early, take her Kiondo, and go to the farm where she would work in the tea estate alongside the workers. And she never forgot her old strip of land in the Old Reserve. Sometimes she made lunch and tea for the workers. This infuriated her husband: why, oh why did she choose to humiliate him before these people? Why would she not conduct herself like a Christian lady? After all, had she not come from a Christian home? Need she dirty her hands now, he asked her, and with labourers too? On clothes, she gave in: she put on shoes and a white hat especially when going to Church. But work was in her bones and this she would not surrender. She enjoyed the touch of the soil: she enjoyed the free and open conversation with the workers.

They liked her. But they resented her husband. Livingstone thought them a lazy lot: why would they not work as hard as he himself had done? Which employer's wife had ever brought him food in a shamba? Miriamu was spoiling them and he told her so.

Occasionally he would look at their sullen faces: he would then remember the days of the Emergency or earlier when he received insults from Ciana employers. But gradually he learnt to silence these unsettling moments in prayer and devotion. He was aware of their silent hatred but thought this a natural envy of the idle and the poor for the rich.

Their faces brightened only in Miriamu's presence. They would abandon their guarded selves and joke and laugh and sing. They gradually let her into their inner lives. They were members of a secret sect that believed that Christ suffered and died for the poor. They called theirs *The Religion of Sorrows*. When her husband was on his business tours, she would attend some of their services. A strange band of men and women: they sang songs they themselves had created and used drums, guitars, jingles and tambourines, producing a throbbing powerful rhythm that made her want to dance with happiness. Indeed they themselves danced around, waving hands in the air, their faces radiating warmth and assurance, until they reached a state of possession and heightened awareness. Then they would speak in tongues strange and beautiful. They seemed united in a common labour and faith: this was what most impressed Miriamu. Something would stir in her, some dormant wings would beat with power inside her, and she would go home trembling in expectation. She would wait for her husband and she felt sure that together they could rescue something from a shattered past. But when he came back from his tours, he was still Dodge W. Livingstone, Jr., senior church elder, and a prosperous farmer and timber merchant. She once more became the model wife listening to her husband as he talked business and arithmetic for the day: what contracts he had won, what money he had won and lost, and tomorrow's prospects. On Sunday man and wife would go to church as usual: same joyless hymns, same prayers from set books; same regular visits to brothers and sisters in Christ; the inevitable tea-parties and charity auctions to which Livingstone was a conspicuous contributor. What a nice family everyone said in admiration and respect: he, the successful farmer and timber merchant; and she, the obedient wife who did her duty to God and husband.

One day he came home early. His face was bright – not wrinkled with the usual cares and worries. His eyes beamed with pleasure. Miriamu's heart gave a gentle leap, could this be true? Was the warrior back? She could see him trying to suppress his excitement. But the next moment her heart fell again. He had said it. His father-in-law, Douglas Jones, had invited him, had begged him to visit them at Molo. He whipped out the letter and started reading it aloud. Then he knelt down and praised the Lord, for his mercy and tender understanding. Miriamu could hardly join in the Amen. Lord, Lord, what has hardened my heart so, she prayed and sincerely desired to see the light.

The day of reunion drew near. His knees were becoming weak. He could not hide his triumph. He reviewed his life and saw in it the guiding finger of God. He the boy from the gutter, a mere milk clerk . . . but he did not want to recall the ridiculous young man who wore patched-up trousers and clowned on a bicycle. Could that have been he, making himself the laughing stock of the whole town? He went to Benbros and secured a new Mercedes Benz 220S. This would make people look at him differently. On the day in question, he himself wore a worsted woollen suit, a waistcoat, and carried a folded umbrella. He talked Miriamu into going in an appropriate dress bought from Nairobi Drapers in Government Road. His own mother had been surprised into a frock and shoe-wearing lady. His two sons in their school uniform spoke nothing but English. (They affected to find it difficult speaking Kikuyu, they made so many mistakes.) A nice family, and they drove to Molo. The old man met them. He had aged, with silver hair covering his head, but he was still strong in body. Jones fell on his knees; Livingstone fell on his knees. They prayed and then embraced in tears. Our son, our son. And my grandchildren too. The past was drowned in tears and prayers. But for Miriamu, the past was vivid in the mind.

Livingstone, after the initial jubilations, found that the memories of that interview rankled a little. Not that he was angry with Jones: the old man had been right, of course. He could not imagine himself giving his own daughter to such a ragamuffin of an upstart clerk. Still he wanted that interview erased from memory forever. And suddenly, and again he saw in that revelation the hand of God, he knew the answer. He trembled a little. Why had he not thought of it earlier? He had a long intimate conversation with his father-in-law and then made the proposal. Wedding at the cross. A renewal of the old. Douglas Jones immediately consented. His son had become a true believer. But Miriamu could not see any sense in the scheme. She was ageing. And the Lord had blessed her with two sons. Where was the sin in that? Again they all fell on her. A proper wedding at the cross of Jesus would make their lives complete. Her resistance was broken. They all praised the Lord. God worked in mysterious ways, his wonders to perform.

The few weeks before the eventful day were the happiest in the life of Livingstone. He savoured every second. Even anxieties and difficulties gave him pleasure. That this day would come: a wedding at the cross. A wedding at the cross, at the cross where he had found the Lord. He was young again. He bounced in health and a sense of well-being. The day he would exchange rings at the cross would erase unsettling memories of yesterday. Cards were printed and immediately despatched. Cars and buses were lined up. He dragged Miriamu to Nairobi. They went from shop to shop all over the city: Kenyatta Avenue, Muindi Bingu Streets, Bazaar, Government Road, Kimathi Street, and back again to Kenyatta Avenue. Eventually he bought her a snow-white long-sleeved satin dress, a veil, white gloves, white shoes and stockings and of course plastic roses. He consulted Rev. Clive Schomberg's still modern classic on good manners for Africans and he hardly departed from the rules and instructions in the matrimonial section. Dodge W. Livingstone, Jr. did not want to make a mistake.

Miriamu did not send or give invitation cards to anybody. She daily prayed that God would give her the strength to go through the whole affair. She wished that the day would come and vanish as in a dream. A week before the day, she was driven all the way back to her parents. She was a mother of two; she was no longer the young girl who once eloped; she simply felt ridiculous pretending that she was a virgin maid at her father's house. But she submitted almost as if she were driven by a power stronger than man. Maybe she was wrong, she thought. Maybe everybody else was right. Why then should she ruin the happiness of many? For even the church was very happy. He, a successful timber merchant, would set a good example to others. And many women had come to congratulate her on her present luck in such a husband. They wanted to share in her happiness. Some wept.

The day itself was bright. She could see some of the rolling fields in Molo: the view brought painful memories of her childhood. She tried to be cheerful. But attempts at smiling only brought out tears: What of the years of waiting? What of the years of hope? Her face-wrinkled father was a sight to see: a dark suit with tails, a waist jacket, top hat and all. She inclined her head to one side, in shame. She prayed for yet more strength: she hardly recognized anybody as she was led towards the holy aisle. Not even her fellow workers, members of the *Religion of Sorrows*, who waited in a group among the crowd outside.

But for Livingstone this was the supreme moment. Sweeter than vengeance. All his life he had slaved for this hour. Now it had come. He had specially dressed for the occasion: a dark suit, tails, top hat and a beaming smile at any dignitary he happened to recognize, mostly MPs, priests and businessmen. The church, Livingstone had time to note, was packed with very important people. Workers and not so important people sat outside. Members of the *Religion of Sorrows* wore red wine-coloured dresses and had with them their guitars, drums and tambourines. The bridegroom as he passed gave them a rather sharp glance. But only for a second. He was really happy.

Miriamu now stood before the cross: her head was hidden in the white veil. Her heart pounded. She saw in her mind's eye a grandmother pretending to be a bride with a retinue of aged bridesmaids. The Charade. The Charade. And she thought: there were ten virgins when the bridegroom came. And five of them were wise – and five of them were foolish – Lord, Lord that this cup would soon be over – over me, and before I be a slave ... and the priest was saying: 'Dodge W. Livingstone, Jr., do you accept this woman for a wife in sickness and health until death do you part?' 'Livingstone's answer was a clear and loud yes. It was now her turn; ... Lord that this cup ... this cup ... over meeeee. ... 'Do you Miriamu accept this man for a husband. ... She tried to answer. Saliva blocked her throat ... five virgins ... five virgins ... came bridegroom ... groom ... and the Church was now silent in fearful expectation.

Suddenly, from outside the Church, the silence was broken. People turned their eyes to the door. But the adherents of the *Religion of Sorrows* seemed unaware of the consternation on people's faces. Maybe they thought the ceremony was over. Maybe they were seized by the spirit. They beat their drums, they beat their tambourines, they plucked their guitars all in a jazzy bouncing unison. Church stewards rushed out to stop them, ssh, ssh, the wedding ceremony was not yet over – but they were way beyond hearing. Their voices and faces were raised to the sky, their feet were rocking the earth.

For the first time Miriamu raised her head. She remembered vaguely that she had not even invited her friends. How had they come to Molo? A spasm of guilt. But only for a time. It did not matter. Not now. The vision had come back ... At the cross, at the cross where I found the Lord ... she saw Wariuki standing before her even as he used to be in Molo. He rode a bicycle: he was playing his tricks before a huge crowd of respectful worshippers ... At the cross, at the cross where I found the Lord ... he was doing it for her ... he had singled only her out of the thrilling throng ... of this she was certain ... came the dancing

and she was even more certain of his love ... He was doing it
for her. Lord, I have been loved once ... once ... I have been
loved, Lord ... And those moments in Ilmorog forest and
woods were part of her: what a moaning, oh, Lord what a moaning ... and the drums and the tambourines were now moaning in
her dancing heart. She was truly Miriamu. She felt so powerful
and strong and raised her head even more proudly; ... and the
priest was almost shouting: 'Do you Miriamu ...' The crowd
waited. She looked at Livingstone, she looked at her father,
and she could not see any difference between them. Her voice
came in a loud whisper: 'No.'

A current went right through the church. Had they heard the
correct answer? And the priest was almost hysterical: 'Do you
Miriamu ...' Again the silence made even more silent by the
singing outside. She lifted the veil and held the audience with
her eyes. 'No, I cannot ... I cannot marry Livingstone ...
because ... because ... I have been married before. I am
married to ... to ... Wariuki ... and he is dead.'

Livingstone became truly a stone. Her father wept. Her mother
wept. They all thought her a little crazed. And they blamed the
whole thing on these breakaway churches that really worshipped
the devil. No properly trained priest, etc. ... etc. ... And the
men and women outside went on singing and dancing to the beat
of drums and tambourines, their faces and voices raised to the
sky.

A MERCEDES FUNERAL

If you ever find yourself in Ilmorog, don't fail to visit Ilmorog Bar & Restaurant: there you're likely to meet somebody you were once at school with and you can reminisce over old days and learn news of missing friends and acquaintances. The big shots of Chiri District frequent the place, especially on Saturday and Sunday evenings after a game of golf and tennis on the lawn grounds of the once FOR EUROPEANS ONLY Sonia Club a few miles away. But for a litre or two of Tusker or Pilsner they all drive to the more relaxed low-class parts of Ilmorog. Mark you, it is not much of a restaurant; don't go there for chickens-in-baskets and steak cooked in wine; it is famous only for charcoal roasted goat meat and nicely dressed barmaids. And of course, gossip. You sit in a U-shaped formation of red-cushioned sofa seats you'll find in public bars all over Kenya. You talk or you listen. No neutrality of poise and bearing, unless of course you pretend: there's no privacy, unless of course you hire a separate room.

It was there one Saturday evening that I sat through an amusing story. Ever heard of a Mercedes Benz Funeral? The narrator, one of those of our dark-suited brothers with a public opinion just protruding, was talking to a group, presumably his visitors, but loudly for all to hear. A little tipsy he probably was; but his voice at times sounded serious and slightly wrought with emotion. I sipped my frothy beer, I am a city man if you want to know, I cocked my ears and soon I was able to gather the few scattered threads; he was talking of someone who had once or recently worked in a Bar:

. . . not much . . . not much I must confess, he was saying. The

truth of the matter, gentlemen, is that I too had forgotten him.
I would not even have offered to tell you about him except . . .
well . . . except that his name surfaced into sudden importance in
that ridiculous affair – but, gentlemen, you must have read about
it . . . no? Is that so? . . . Anyway the affair was there all right and
it really shook us in Ilmorog. It even got a few inch columns in
the national dailies. And that's something, you know, especially
with so many bigger scandals competing for attention. Big men
fighting it out with fists and wrestling one another to the
ground . . . candidates beaten up by hired thugs . . . others
arrested on nomination day for mysterious reasons and released
the day after, again for mysterious reasons. A record year,
gentlemen, a record year, that one. With such events competing
for attention, why should any one have taken an interest in a
rather silly story of an unknown corpse deciding the outcome of
an election in a remote village town? And yet fact number one . . .
not, gentlemen, that I want to theorize . . . yet the truth is that his
death or rather his funeral would never have aroused so much
heat had it not come during an election year.

Now, let me see, count rather: there was that seat in parliament:
the most Hon. John Joe James . . . would you believe it, used to
be known as John Karanja but dropped his African name on
first being elected . . . standard, efficiency and international
dignity demanded it of him you know . . . anyway he wanted to
be returned unopposed. There was also the leadership of the
party's branch: the chairman . . . wait, his name was Ruoro but he
had been the leader of the branch for so long – no meetings, no
elections, ran the whole thing himself – that people simply
called him the chairman . . . he too wanted a fresh, unopposed
mandate. There were vacancies in the County Council and in
other small bodies, too numerous to mention. But all the
previous occupants wanted to be returned with increased majori-
ties, unopposed. Why, when you come to think of it, why do a
few out of jobs they had done for six years and more? Specialists
. . . experience . . . all that and more. And why add to unemploy-

ment? Unfortunately there were numerous upstarts who had different ideas and wanted a foot and a hand in running the very same jobs. Dynamism ... fresh blood ... all that and more. Naturally gentlemen, and I am sure this was also true in your area, the job which most thought they could execute with unique skill and efficiency was that of The Hon. M.P. for Ilmorog. See what I mean? More Tusker beer gentlemen? Hey sister ... sister ... these barmaids! ... baada ya kazi jiburudishe na Tusker.

Well, after the first round of trial runs and feelers through a whispering campaign, the field was left to the incumbent and three challengers. There was the university student ... you know the sort you find these days ... a Lumumba goatee ... weather-beaten American shirts and jeans ... they dress only in foreign clothes ... foreign fashions ... foreign ideas ... you remember our time in Makerere under De Bunsen? Worsted woollen suits, starched white shirts and ties to match ... now that's what I call proper dressing ... anyway, our student challenger claimed to be an intellectual worker and as such could fully understand the aspirations of all workers. There was also an aspiring businessman. An interesting case this one. Had just acquired a loan to build a huge self-service supermarket here in Ilmorog shopping centre. It was whispered that he had diverted a bit of that loan into his campaign. He would tell his audience that man was born to make money: if he went to parliament, he would ensure that everybody had a democratic chance to make a little pile. He himself would set an example: a leader must lead. Also in the arena was a Government Chief, or rather ex-Chief, who had resigned his job to enter the race. He claimed that he would make a very good chief in parliament. Sweat and sacrifice, he used to say, were ever his watchwords. As an example of S and S, he had not only given up a very promising career in the civil service to offer himself as a complete servant of the people, but had also sold three of his five grade cows to finance his campaign. His wife protested of course, but

... sister, I asked you for some beer ... we all have our weak-
nesses, eh?

Each challenger denounced the other two accusing them of
splitting the votes. If they, the other two that is, were sincere,
would they not do the honourable thing, stand down in favour
of one opponent? The three were however united in denouncing
the sitting member: what had he done for the area? He had only
enriched himself and his relatives. They pointed to his business
interests, his numerous buildings in the area, and his many
shares in even the smallest Petrol Station in the Constituency.
From what forgotten corner had he suddenly acquired all that
wealth, including a thousand-acre farm, asked the aspiring
businessman? Why had he not given others a democratic chance
to dip a hand in the common pool? The student demanded:
what has he done for we Wafanyi Kazi? The ex-Chief accused
him of never once visiting his constituency. His election had
been a one-way ticket to the city. They all chorused: let the
record speak, let the record speak for itself. Funnily enough
gentlemen, the incumbent replied with the same words – yes, let
the record speak – but managed to give them a tone of great
achievement. First he pointed out what the government had
done ... the roads ... hospitals ... factories ... tourist hotels
and resorts ... Hilton, the Intercontinental and all that. Anybody
who said the government had done nothing for Wananchi was
demagogic and indulging in cheap politics. To the charge that he
was not a Minister and hence was not in government, he would
laugh and flywhisk away such ignorance. From where did the
government derive its strength and power? From among whom
was the Cabinet chosen? To the charge that he had made it, he
answered by accusing the others of raging with envy and con-
genital idleness ... a national cake on the table ... some people
too lazy or too fat to lift a finger and take a piece ... waited to
have it put into their mouths and chewed for them, even. To the
ex-Chief he said: didn't this would-be-M.P. ... a man without
any experience ... didn't he know that the job of an M.P. was to

attend parliament and make good laws that hanged thieves, repatriated vagabonds and prostitutes back to the rural areas? You don't make laws by sitting in your home drinking Chang'aa and playing draughts. For the student he had only scornful laughter: intellectual workers ... he means intellectuals whose one speciality is stoning other people's cars and property! Gentlemen ... there was nothing in the campaign, no issues, no ideas ... just promises. People were bored. They did not know whom to choose although the non-arguments of the aspiring businessman held more sway. You, your bottle is still empty ... you want a change to something stronger? Vat 69? No? ... oh ... oh ... Chang'aa, did you say? Ha! ha! ha! ... Chang'aa for power ... Kill-me-Quick ... no, that is never in stock here ... sister, hey sister ... another round ... the same.

You mention Chang'aa. Actually it was Chang'aa, you might say, that saved the campaign. Put it this way. If Wahinya, the other watchman in Ilmorog Bar and Restaurant, had not suddenly died of alcoholic poisoning, our village, our town would never have been mentioned in any daily. Wahinya dead became the most deadly factor in the election. It was during a rather diminished public meeting addressed by the candidates that the student shouted something about 'We Workers'. The others took up the challenge. They too were workers. Everybody, said the incumbent, everybody was a worker except the idle, the crippled, prostitutes and students. A man from the audience stood up. By now people had lost their original awe and curiosity and respect for the candidates. Anyway this man stands up. He was a habitual drunk – and that day he must have broken a can or two. Who cares about the poor worker, he asked, imitating in turn the oratorical gestures of each speaker. These days the poor die and don't even have a hole in which to be put, leave alone a burial in a decent coffin. People laughed, applauding. They could well understand this man's concern for he himself, skin and bones only, looked on the verge of the grave. But he stood his ground and mentioned the case of Wahinya. His words had an electric effect.

That night all the candidates singly and secretly went to the wife of the deceased and offered to arrange for Wahinya's funeral.

Now I don't know if this be true in your area, but in our village funerals had become a society affair, our version of cocktail parties. I mean since Independence. Before 1952, you know before the Emergency, the body would be put away in puzzled silence and tears. People, you see, were awed by death. But they confronted it because they loved life. They asked: what's death? because they wanted to know what was life! They came to offer sympathy and solidarity to the living and helped in the burial. A pit. People took turns to dig it in ritual silence. Then the naked body was lowered into the earth. A little soil was first sprinkled over it. The body, the earth, the soil: what was the difference? Then came the Emergency. Guns on every side. Fathers, mothers, children, cattle, donkeys – all killed, and bodies left in the open for vultures and hyenas. Or mass burial. People became cynical about death: they were really indifferent to life. You today: me tomorrow. Why cry my Lord? Why mourn the dead? There was only one cry: for the victory of the struggle. The rest was silence. What do you think, gentlemen? Shall we ever capture that genuine respect for death in an age where money is more important than life? Today what is left? A showbiz. Status. Even poor people will run into debts to have the death of a relative announced on the radio and funeral arrangements advertised in the newspapers. And gossip, gentlemen, the gossip. How many attended the funeral? How much money was collected? What of the coffin? Was the pit cemented? Plastic flowers: plastic tears. And after a year, every year there is an Ad. addressed to the dead.

IN LOVING MEMORY. A YEAR HAS PASSED BUT TO US IT IS JUST LIKE TODAY WHEN YOU SUDDENLY DEPARTED FROM YOUR LOVED ONES WITHOUT LETTING THEM KNOW OF YOUR LAST WISH. DEAR, YOU HAVE ALWAYS BEEN A GUIDING STAR, A STAR THAT WILL ALWAYS SHINE, etc., etc.

You see, our man was right. It was a disgrace to die poor: even the Church will not receive the poor in state, though the priest will rush to the death-bed to despatch the wretch quickly on a heaven-bound journey, and claim another victim for Christ. So you see where Wahinya's death, a poor worker's death, comes in!

I don't know how far this is true, but it is said that each candidate would offer the wife money if she would leave all the funeral arrangements and oration in their sole hands ... You say, she should have auctioned the rights? Probably ... probably. But those were only rumours. What I do know for a fact, well, a public fact, was that the wife and her husband's body suddenly vanished. Stolen, you say? In a way, yes. It was rumoured that J.J.J. had had a hand in it. The others called a public meeting to denounce the act. How could anybody steal a dead body? How dare a leader show so little respect for the dead and the feelings of the public? The crowd must also have felt cheated of a funeral drama. They shouted: Produce the body: produce the body! The meeting became so hot and near-riotous that the police had to be called. But even then the tempers could not be cooled. The body, the body, they shouted. J.J.J., normally the very picture of calmness, wiped his face once or twice. It was the student who saved the day: he suggested setting up a committee not only to investigate the actual disappearance but to go into the whole question of poor men's funerals. All the contestants were elected members of the committee. Well, and a few neutrals. There was a dispute as to who would chair the committee's meetings. The burden fell on the chairman of the branch. Thereafter all the candidates tried to please him. Rumours became even more rife. Gangs of supporters followed the committee and roamed through the villages. And now the miracle of miracles. As suddenly as she had disappeared, Wahinya's wife now surfaced and would not disclose where she had been. More, the body had found its way to the City Mortuary. This started even more rumours. No beer-party was complete without a story relating to the affair. Verbal bulletins on the deliberations of the committee were daily released and became the talking points in all the bars. People, through the chairman, were kept informed of every detail about the funeral arrangements. Overnight, so to speak, Wahinya had, so to speak, risen from the dead to be the most powerful factor in the elections. People whispered: who is this Wahinya? Details of his life were unearthed: numerous people claimed special acquaintance and told alluring stories about him. Dead, he was larger than life. Dead, he was everybody's closest friend.

Me? Yes, gentlemen, me too. I had actually met him on three different occasions: when he was a porter, then as a turn-boy and more recently as a watchman. And I can say this: Wahinya's progress from hope to a drinking despair is the story of our time. But what is the matter, gentlemen? You are not drinking? Sister, hey, sister . . . see to these gentlemen . . . well, never mind . . . as soon as they finish this round . . . Yes, gentlemen . . . to drink, to be merry . . . Life is – but no theories I promised you . . . no sermons, although I will say this again: Wahinya's rather rapid progress towards the grave is really the story of our troubled times!

There was a long pause in the small hall. I tried to sip my beer, but half-way I put the glass back on the table. I was not alone. Half-full glasses of stale beer stood untouched all round. Everybody must have been listening to the story. The narrator, a glass of beer in his hand, stared pensively at the ground, and somehow in that subdued atmosphere his public opinion seemed less offensive. He put the glass down and his voice when it came seemed to have been affected by the attentive silence:

I first came to know him fairly well in the 1960s, he started. Those, if you remember, were the years when dreams like garden perfume in the wind wafted through the air of our villages. The years, gentlemen, when rumours of Uhuru made people's hearts palpitate with fearful joy of what would happen tomorrow: if something should – ? But no – nothing untoward would possibly bar the coming of that day, the opening of the gate. Imagine: to elect our sons spokesmen of black power, after so much blood . . . so much blood . . . !

He too, you can guess, used to dream. Beautiful dreams about the future. I imagine that even while sagging under the weight of sacks of sugar, sacks of maize flour, sacks of magadi salt and soda, he would be in a world all his own. Flower fields of green peas and beans. Gay children chasing nectar-seeking bees and butterflies. A world to visit, a world to conquer. Wait till tomorrow, my Lord, till tomorrow. He was tall and frail-looking but strong with clear dark eyes that lit up with hope. And you can imagine that at such times the sack of sugar would feel light on his back, his limbs would acquire renewed strength, he was the giant in the story who could pull mountains by the roots or blow trees into the sky with his rancid breath. Trees, roots, branches and all flew into the sky high, high, no longer trees but feathers carried by the wind. Fly away, bird, little one of the courtyard and come again to gather millet grains in the sand. He would lay down the sack to watch the bird fly into the unknown and no doubt his dreams would also soar even beyond the present sky, his soul's eye would scan hazier and hazier horizons hiding away knowledge of tomorrow. But from somewhere in the shop a shout from his Indian employer would haul him back to this earth. Hurry up with that load, you lazy boy. Money you want, work no! You think money coming from dust or fall from sky. Kumanyoko. No doubt Wahinya would sigh. He was after all only a porter in Shukla and Shukla Stores, an object like that very load against which he had been leaning.

Shukla and Shukla: that's where I used to meet him. I was then a student in Siriana boarding school. A missionary affair it was in those days, I mean the school and its numerous rules and restrictions. For instance, we were never allowed out of the school compound except on Saturday afternoons and even then not

beyond a three-mile radius. Chura township, a collection of a
dozen Indian-owned shops and a post office, was the only centre
within our limits, both physical and financial. With ten cents,
fifty cents or a shilling in our pockets, we used to walk there with
determination as if on a very important mission. An unhurried
stroll around the shops . . . then a Fanta soda, or a few madhvani
gummy sweets from Shukla and Shukla . . . and, our day was
over. Well, I used never to have more than two shillings pocket
money for a whole term. So I would often go to Chura without a
hope of crowning my Saturday afternoon outing with Fantas,
madazis or madhvanis. A sweet, a soft drink was then a world.
You laugh. But do you know how I envied those who strode that
world with showy impunity and suggestions of even greater
well-being at their homes? As soon as I reached the stores,
friends and foes had to be avoided. I lied and I knew they knew
I lied when I pretended having important business further on.
Still, can you imagine the terror in case I was found out and
exposed?

Wahinya must have seen through me. I can't remember how
we first met or who first spoke to whom. I remember, though,
my initial embarrassment at his ragged clothes and his grimy
face. It seemed he might pull me down to his level. What would
the other boys think of me? How quickly school could separate
people! At home in order to preserve my school uniform I wore
similarly ragged clothes and often went to bed hungry. From our
conversations I soon found that we shared a common back-
ground. We came from Ilmorog. We were both without fathers:
mine had died of Chang'aa poisoning: his had died whilst
fighting in the forest. So we were brought up by mothers who
had to scratch the dry earth for a daily can of unga and for fees.
We attended similar types of Primary Schools: Karing's Independent. But while mine came under the Colonial District
Education Board, his was closed and the building burnt down
by the British. All African-run schools were suspected of aiding
in the freedom struggle.

Thus blind chance had put Wahinya and me on different paths. And yet with all our shared past, I felt slightly above him, superior. Deep in my stomach was the terror that he might besmirch my standing in school. But occasionally he would slip twenty cents or fifty cents into my hands. For this I was grateful and it of course softened my initial repugnance. So I, the recipient of his hard-earned cents that helped me hide my humiliation of lies and pretence and put me on an equal footing with the other boarders, became the recipient of his dreams, ambitions and plans for the future.

'You are very lucky,' Wahinya would always start, his eyes lit. He would then tell me how he loved school and what positions he had held in the various classes. 'From Kiai to Standard 4, I was never below No. 3. Especially English ... aah, nobody could beat me in that ... and in history ... you remember that African king we learnt about? What was his name ... Chaka, and Moshoeshoe ... and how they fought the British with stones, spears and bare hands ... and Waiyaki, the Laibon, Mwanga, the Nandi struggle against the British army ...' He would become excited. He would reel off name after name of the early African heroes. But for me now educated at Siriana this was not history. I pitied him really. I wanted to tell him about the true and correct history: the Celts, the Anglo-Saxons, the Danes and Vikings, William the Conqueror, Drake, Hawkins, Wilberforce, Nelson, Napoleon, and all these real heroes of history. But then I thought he would not understand secondary school history and Siriana was reputed to have the best and toughest education. He would not, in any case, let me slip in a word. For he was now back with his heroes gazing at today and tomorrow: 'Do they teach you that kind of history in Siriana? Only it must be harder to understand ... I used to draw sketches of all the battles ... the teacher liked them ... he made me take charge of the blackboard ... you know, duster, chalk and the big ruler in the shape of a T. You know it?' He would question me about Siriana: what subject, what kind of teachers ... 'Europeans, eh?

Do they beat you? Is it difficult learning under whitemen who speak English through the nose?' Often as he spoke he would be eyeing my jacket and green tie: he would touch the badge with the school motto in Latin and I often had the feeling that he enjoyed Siriana through me. I was the symbol of what he would soon become, especially with the rumoured departure of white-men.

And that, gentlemen, was how I would always like to remember Wahinya: a boy who had never lost his dreams for higher education. His eyes would often acquire a distant look, misty even, and he seemed impatient with his present Shukla sur-roundings and the slow finger of time. 'This work . . . only for a time now . . . a few more days . . . a little bit more money . . . aah, school again . . . you think I will be able to do it? . . . Our teacher . . . he was a good one . . . used to make us sing songs . . . I had a good voice . . . you should hear it one day . . . he used to tell us: boys don't gaze in wonder at the things the whiteman has made: pins, guns, bombs, aeroplanes . . . what one man can do, another one can . . . what one race can do, another one can, and more . . . One day . . . but never mind!' He always cut short the reference to his teacher, his eyes would become even more misty and for a few seconds he would not speak to me. Then as if defying fate itself, he would re-affirm his teacher's maxim: what one man can do, another one can. Newspapers, well, printed words fascinated him. He always carried in his pockets an old edition of *The Standard* and in between one job and the next he would struggle to spell out words and meanings. 'You think one day I'll be able to read this? I want to be able to read it blindfolded, even. Read it through the nose, eh? Now you see me stumbling over all these words. But one day I will read it . . . easy . . . like swallowing water . . . Here tell me the meaning of this word . . . de . . . de . . . deadlo . . . ck . . . deadlock . . . how can a lock die?' I must say I could not help being affected by his enthusiasm and his unbounded faith especially in those days of lean pockets and occasional gunsmoke in the sky.

Gentlemen, you are no longer touching your drinks. What's left to us but to drink? Drinking dulls ones fear and terror and memories ... and yet I cannot forget the last time I saw him in Chura. Same kind of Saturday afternoon. He was waiting for me by the railway crossing. I was embarrassed by this and I affected a casual approach and cool words. He was excited. He walked beside me, tried the customary pleasantries, then whipped out something from his pocket. An old edition of *The Standard*. 'See this ... see this,' he said opening a page ... 'Read it, read it,' he said thrusting the whole thing into my hands. But still he tried to read over my shoulder as we walked towards Shukla and Shukla stores.

Did you miss the student airlift abroad?
Study abroad while at home.
Opportunities for higher education.
Opportunities for an attractive career.
All through correspondence.
Apply:
Quick Results College,
Bristol,
England.
P.S. We cater for anything from primary to university.

It was the days of those airlifts to America and Europe, you remember. Wahinya was capering around me. He fired many questions at me. But I knew nothing about correspondence schools. I dared not show him my ignorance though. I tried to make disparaging comments about learning through the post. But he was not really interested in my defeatist answers. His dream of higher education would soon be realized. 'I can manage it ... I will manage it ... Uhuru is coming, you see, ... Uhuru ... more and better jobs ... more money ... might even own part of Shukla and Shukla ... for these Indians are going to go, you know ... money ... but what I want is this thing: I must one day read *The Standard* through the nose ...' I left him standing by Shukla and Shukla, peering at *The Standard*, his eyes probably blazing a trail that led to a future with dignity. Nothing, it seemed, would ever break his faith, his hopes, his dreams, and that in a land that had yet to recover from guns, concentration camps and broken homes.

I went back to my studies and prepared for the coming exams. Most of us got through and were accepted in Makerere, then the only University College in East Africa . . . no – not quite true . . . there was Dar es Salaam . . . but then it had only started. No more fees. No more rules and restrictions. We wore worsted gaberdines and smoked and danced. We even had pocket money. Uhuru also came to our countries. We sang and danced and wept. Tomorrow. Cha. Cha. Cha. Uhuru. Cha. Cha. Cha. We streamed into the streets of Kampala. We linked hands and chanted: Uhuru. Cha. Cha. Cha. It was a kind of collective madness, I remember, and those women with whom we linked our loins knew it and gave themselves true. The story was the same for each of us. But none of us I am quite sure that night fully realized the full import of what had happened. This we knew in the coming years and perhaps Wahinya had been right. And what years, my Lord! Strange things we heard and saw: most of those who had finished Makerere were now being trained as District Officers, Labour Officers, Diplomats, Foreign Service – all European jobs. Uhuru. Cha. Cha. Cha. Others were now on the boards of Shell, Caltex, Esso, and other oil companies. We could hardly wait for our turn. Uhuru. Cha. Cha. Cha. Some came for the delayed graduation ceremonies. They came in their dark suits, their cars and red-lipped ladies in heels. They talked of their jobs, of their cars, of their employees; of their mahogany-furnished offices and of course their European and Asian secretaries. So this was true. No longer the rumours, no longer the unbelievable stories. And we were next in the queue.

We now dreamt not of sweets, Fanta and ginger-ale. The car was now our world. We compared names: VW, DKW, Ford

Prefects, Peugeots, Flying A's. Mercedes Benzes were then beyond the reach of our imagination. Nevertheless, it all seemed a wonder that we would soon be living in European mansions, eat in European hotels, holiday in European resorts at the coast and play golf. And with such prospects before my eyes, how could I remember Wahinya?

Travelling in a bus to the city one Saturday during my last holidays before graduation, I was dreaming of a world that would soon be mine. With a degree in Economics and Commerce, any job in most firms was within my grasp. Houses ... cars ... shares ... land in the settled area ... these whirled through my mind when suddenly I noticed my bus was no longer alone. It was racing with another called *Believe In God No. I*, at a reckless pace. I held my stomach in both hands, as we would say. The two buses were now running parallel making on-coming vehicles rush to a sudden stop by the roadside. It seemed my future was being interfered with by this reckless race to death. And the turn-boys: they banged the body of the bus, urging their driver to accelerate – has the bus caught tuberculosis? – at the same time jeering and hurling curses at the turn-boys of the enemy bus. They would climb to the luggage rack at the top and then swing down, monkey-fashion, to the side. They were playing, toying with death, like the death-riders I once saw in a visiting circus from India. You could touch the high-voltage tension in the bus. At one stage a woman screamed in an orgasm of fear and this seemed to act like a spur on the turn-boys and the driver. Suddenly *Believe in God No. I* managed to pull past and you could now see the dejected look on the turn-boys in our bus, while relief was registered on the faces of the passengers. It was then, when I dared to look, that I saw one of the turn-boys was no other than Wahinya.

He came into the bus, shaking his head from side to side as if in utter unbelief. He was now even more frail looking but his face had matured with hard lines all over. I slunk even further into my seat instinctively avoiding contact. But he must have seen me

because suddenly his eyes were lit up, he rushed towards me
shouting my name for all in the bus to hear. 'My friend, my
friend,' he called, clasping my hands in his and sitting beside me,
slapped me hard on the shoulders. He was much less reserved
than before and despite an attempt to keep the conversation low
his voice rose above the others. 'Still at Makerere? You are lucky,
eh! But remember our days in Chura? Those Indians ... they
never left ... dismissed me just like that ... But it's good our
people are rising ... like the owner of these buses ... the other
day he was a Matatu driver ... now see him, a fleet of ten buses
... In one day he can count over 100,000 shillings ... Not bad,
eh? You better finish school soon, man. Educated people like
you can get loans. You start a business ... like the owner of
these buses ... do you know him? The M.P. for the area ...
John Joe James, or J.J.J. ... To tell you the truth, this is what
I want to do ... a little money ... I buy an old Peugeot ... start
a Matatu ... I tell you no other business can beat transport
business for quick money ... except buying and renting houses
... Driver, more oil,' and suddenly, to my relief I must say, he
stood up and rushed along the unpeopled isle. He had spied
another bus. The race for passengers would start all over.

I went away slightly sad. What had happened to the boy with
hopes for an education abroad while at home? I soon dismissed
this sudden jolt at my own dreams, and tried to re-experience
that sweetness in the soul at the prospect of eating a tasty meal.
But the death-race had dampened my spirits.

Eh? A glass to recover my breath? Welcome, sweet wine ...
Sweet eloquence ... but what's the matter, gentlemen? Drink
also ... I say a good drink, in a way, is the blood of life.

You should have seen us a week after graduation. We drank
ourselves silly. Gates of heaven were now open, because we had
the key ... the key ... open sesame into the world. Mark you it
was not as rosy as it had seemed once we started working. I
worked with a commercial firm and all the important ranks were
filled with whites ... experts, you know ... and one stayed for so

long in training, it tried one's patience ... especially four years after independence ... Is it still the same? In a way yes ... experts who are technically under you and still are paid more ... and make real decisions ... still I can't say I have been disappointed ... If you work hard you can get somewhere ... and with government and bank loans ... the other day I got myself a little shamba ... a thousand acres ... a few hundred cows ... and with a European manager ... the 'garden' is doing all right. And that's how I get a few cents to drink ... now and then ... my favourite bar has always been this one ... gives me a sense of homecoming ... and I can observe things you know ... homeboy ... after all man has ambitions ... And occasionally they employ beautiful juicy barmaids ... man must live ... mustn't he? There was one here ... huge behind ... Mercedes they used to call her ... I prefer them big ... anyway one day I wanted her so bad. I winked at the watchman. I bent down to scribble a note on the back of the bill: would she be free tonight? Then I raised my head. The watchman stood in front of me. He had on a huge kabuti, with a kofia and a bokora-club clutched firmly in his hands. This was a new one I thought. Then our eyes met. Lo! It was Wahinya.

He hesitated that one second. A momentary indecision. 'Wahinya?' It was I who called out, automatically stretching my hand. He took my hand and replied rather formally, 'Yes, Sir,' but I did detect the suggestion of an ironic smile at the edges of his mouth. 'Don't you remember me?' 'I do,' but there was no recognition in his voice or in his manner. 'What did you want?' he asked, politely. My heart fell. I was now embarrassed. 'Have a drink on me?' 'I will have the bill sent to you. But if you don't mind, we are not allowed to drink while customers are in, so I will take it later.' And he went back to his post. I had not the courage to give him the note. I went home, driving my Mercedes 220S furiously through the dark. What could I do for the man? What had happened to his dreams? ... broken and there was not the slightest sparkle in his eyes. And yet the next weekend I was

back there. That barmaid. Her whole body looked like the juicy
thing itself crying: do it to me, do it to me. But whom could I
send? I again called out for the watchman. I argued; he was after
all employed for little services like that. And he was taking
messages for others, wasn't he? I gave him the note and nodded
in the direction of the fat barmaid. He smiled, no light in his eyes,
with that mechanical studied understanding of his job and what
was required of him. He came back with a note: 'YES: Room 14.
CASH.' I gave him twenty shillings and well, how could I help it,
a tip . . . a tip of two shillings . . . which he accepted with the
same mechanical precision. Wahinya! Reduced to a carrier of
secrets between men and women!

Occasionally he would come to work drunk and you could
tell this by the feverish look in his eyes. He would talk and
even boast of all the women he had had, of the amount of drink
he could hold. Then he would crawl with his voice and ask for a
few coins to buy a cigarette. I soon came to learn how he lost his
job of a turn-boy. His bus and another collided while racing for
a cargo of passengers. A number of people died including the
driver. He himself was severely injured. When he came back
from the hospital, there was no job for him. J.J.J. would not
even give him a little compensation . . . he would talk on like
that as in a delirium. And yet when he had not taken a drop, he
was very quiet and very withdrawn into his kofia and kabuti.
But as weeks and months passed, the sober moments became
rarer and rarer. He became a familiar figure in the bar. At times
he would drink all his salary in credit so that at the end of the
month he was forced to beg for a glass or fifty cents. He had
already started on Kiruru and Chang'aa. At such moments, he
would be full of drunken dreams and impossible schemes.
'Don't worry . . . I will die in a Mercedes Benz . . . don't laugh
. . . I will save, go into business, and then buy one . . . easy . . .
the moment I buy one, I will stop working. I will live and die
like Lord Delamare.' People baptized him Wahinya Benji. Often,
I wondered if he ever remembered the old days in Chura.

One Saturday night he came and sat beside me. This boldness surprised me because he was very sober. I offered him a drink. He refused. His voice was level, subdued, but a bit of the old sparkle was in his eyes.

'You now see me a wreck. But I often ask myself: could it have been different? With a chance – an education, like yours. You remember our days in Chura? Aah, a long time ago . . . another world . . . that correspondence school, do you remember it? Well, I never got the money. And it was harder later saddled with a wife and a child. Mark you, it was a comfort. Aah, but a little money . . . a little more education . . . school . . . our teacher . . . you remember him? I used to talk to you about him. What for instance he used to tell us? What one man can do, another one can: What one race can do, another one can . . . Do you think this true? You have an education: you have got Makerere: you might even go to England to get a degree like the son of Koinange. Tell me this: is that really true? Is it true for us ordinary folk who can't speak a word of English? Put it this way: I am not afraid of hard work; I am not scared of sweating. He used to tell us: after Uhuru, we must work hard: Europeans are where they are because they work hard: and what one man can do, another one can. He was a good man, all the same, used to tell us about great Africans. Then one day . . . one day . . . you see, we were all in school . . . and then some whitemen came, Johnnies, and took him out of our classroom. We climbed the mud-walls in fear. A few yards away they roughly pushed him forward and shot him dead.'

Wahinya's drinking became so bad that he was dismissed from his job. And I never really saw him in that ruined state because my duties with the Progress Bank International took me outside the country. But even now as I talk, I feel his presence around me, his boasts, his dreams, his drinking and well, that last encounter.

The narrator swallowed one or two glasses in quick succession.

I followed his example. It was as if we all had witnessed a nasty scene and we wanted to drown the memory of it. The narrator after a time tried to break the sombre atmosphere with exaggerated unconcern and cynicism: 'You see the twists of fate, gentlemen, Wahinya dead had become prominent, even J.J.J. his former employer was fighting for him,' but he could not deceive anybody. He could not quite recapture the original tone of light entertainment. There was after all the Chura episode behind us. Wahinya, whom I had never met but whom I felt I knew, had come back to haunt our drinking peace. Somebody said: 'It's a pity he never got his Mercedes Benz – at least a ride.'

You are wrong, said the narrator. In a way, he got that too. You shake your heads, gentlemen? Give us a drink, sister, give us another one.

It was all thanks to the rivalry among the candidates. Although they were all members of the committee charged with burial arrangements, they would not agree to a joint effort. Each you see wanted only his own plan adopted. Each wanted his name mentioned as the sole donor of something. After one or two riotous sessions, the committee finally decided on a broad policy.

Item No. 1. Money. It was decided that the amount each would give would be disclosed and announced on the actual day of the funeral.

Item No. 2. Transport. J.J.J. had offered what he described as his wife's shopping basket, a brand-new, light-green Cortina G.T., to carry the body from the city mortuary, but the others objected. So it was decided that the four would contribute equal amounts towards the hire of a neutral car – a Peugeot family saloon.

Item No. 3. The Pit. Again the four would share the expenses of digging and cementing it.

Item No. 4. The coffin and the cross. On this they would not agree to a joint contribution. Each wanted to be the sole donor of the coffin and the cross. Mark you, none of them was a known believer. A compromise: they were to contribute to a neutral coffin to transport the body from the mortuary, to the church and to the cemetery. But each would bring his own coffin and cross and the crowd would choose the best. Participatory democracy, you see.

Item No. 5. Funeral Oration. Five minutes for each candidate before presenting his coffin and the cross.

Item No. 6. Day. Even on this, there was quite a haggling. But a Sunday was thought the most appropriate day.

That was a week that was, gentlemen. Every night, every bar was full to capacity with people who had come to gather gossip and rumours. Market-days burst with people. In buses there was no other talk; the turn-boys had field-days regaling passengers with tales of Wahinya. No longer the merits and demerits of the various candidates: issues in any case there had been none. Now only Wahinya and the funeral.

On the Sunday in question, believers and non-believers, Protestants, Catholics, Muslims, and one or two recent converts to Radha Krishnan flocked to Ilmorog Presbyterian Church. For the first time in Ilmorog, all the bars, even those that specialized in illegal Chang'aa, were empty. A ghost town Ilmorog was that one Sunday morning. Additional groups came from villages near and far. Some from very distant places had hired buses and lorries. Even the priest, Rev. Bwana Solomon, who normally would not receive bodies of non-active members into the holy building unless of course they were rich and prominent, this time arrived early in resplendent dark robes laced with silver and gold. A truly memorable service, especially the beautifully trembling voice of Rev. Solomon as he intoned: 'Blessed are the meek and poor for they shall inherit the earth: blessed are those who mourn for they shall be comforted.' After the service, we trooped on foot, in cars, on lorries, in buses to the graveyard where we found even more people seated. Fortunately loudspeakers had been fixed through the thoughtful kindness of the District

Officer so that even those at the far outer edges could clearly hear the speeches and funeral orations. After the prayers, again Rev. Solomon with his beautifully trembling voice captured many hearts, the amount of money each candidate had donated was announced.

The businessman had given seven hundred and fifty shillings. The farmer had given two hundred and fifty. J.J.J. had given one thousand. Oh hearing this the businessman rushed back to the microphone to announce an additional three hundred. A murmur of general approval greeted the businessman's additional gift. Lastly the student. He had given only twenty shillings.

What we all waited for with bated breath was the gift of coffins and crosses. There was a little dispute as to who would open the act. Each wanted to have the last word. Lots were cast. The student, the farmer, the businessman and J.J.J. followed in that order.

The student tugged at his Lumumba goatee. He lashed at wealth and ostentatious living. He talked about workers. Simplicity and hard work. That should be our national motto. And in keeping with that motto, he had arranged for a simple wooden coffin and wooden cross. After all Jesus had been a carpenter. A few people jeered as the student stepped down.

Then came the farmer. He too believed in simplicity and hard work. He believed in the soil. As a government chief he had always encouraged Wananchi in their patriotic efforts at farming. His was also a simple wooden affair but with a slight variation. He had already hired the services of one of the popular artists who painted murals or mermaids in our bars, to paint a picture of a green cow with udders and teats ripeful with milk. There was amused laughter from the crowd.

What would the businessman bring us? He, in his dark suit with a protruding belly, rose to the occasion and the heightened expectations. People were not to be bothered that a few had never had it so good. What was needed was a democratic chance for all the Wahinyas of this world. A chance to make a

little pile so that on dying they might leave their widows and
orphans decent shelters. He called out his followers. They
unfolded the coffin. It was truly an elaborate affair. It was built
in the shape of a Hilton hotel complete with stories and glass
windows. Whistles of admiration and satisfaction at the new turn
in the drama came from the crowd. His followers unfolded the
cloth: an immaculate white sheet that elicited more whistling of
amused approval. The businessman then stepped down with the
air of a sportsman who has broken a long-standing record and
set a new one that could not possibly be ever equalled.

Now everyone waited for J.J.J. His six years in parliament
had made him an accomplished actor. He took his time. His
leather briefcase with bulging papers was there: he collected his
ivory walking stick and flywhisk. His belly though big was right
for his height. He talked about his long service and experience.
People did not in the old days send an uncircumcised boy to lead
a national army, he said slightly glancing at the opponents ...
He had always fought for the poor. But he would not bore people
with a long talk on such a sad occasion. He did not want to
bring politics into what was a human loss. All he wanted was not
only to pay his respects to the dead but also to respect the wishes
of the dead. Now before Wahinya died, he was often heard to
say ... but wait! This was the right cue for his followers. The
coffin was wrapped in a brilliantly red cloth. Slowly they
unfolded it. People in the crowd were now climbing the backs
of others in order to see, to catch a glimpse of this thing. Suddenly there was an instinctive gasp from the crowd when at last
they saw the coffin raised high. It was not a coffin at all, but
really an immaculate model of a black Mercedes Benz 660S
complete with doors and glasses and maroon curtains and
blinds.

He let the impact made by this revelation run its full course.
Only the respect for the dead, he continued as if nothing had
happened. Before Brother Wahinya had died, he had spoken of
a wish of dying in a Benz. His last wish: I say let's respect the

wishes of the dead. He raised his flywhisk to greet the expected applause'while holding a white handkerchief to his eyes.

But somehow no applause came; not even a murmur of approval. Something had gone wrong, and we all felt it. It was like an elaborate joke that had suddenly misfired. Or as if we had all been witnesses of an indecent act on a public place. The people stood and started moving away as if they did not want to be identified with the indecency. J.J.J., his challengers and a few of their hired followers were left standing by the pit, no doubt wondering what had gone wrong. Suddenly J.J.J. returned to his own car and drove off. The others quickly left.

Wahinya was buried by relatives and friends in a simple coffin which, of course, had been blessed by Rev. Solomon.

About the elections, the outcome I mean, there is little to tell. You know that J.J.J. is still in Parliament. There were the usual rumours of rigging, etc., etc. The student got a hundred votes and returned to school. I believe he graduated, a degree in commerce, and like me joined a bank. He got a loan, bought houses from non-citizen Indians and he is now a very important landlord in the city. A European-owned estate agency takes care of the houses.

The businessman was ruined. He had dug too deep a pit into the loan money. His shop and a three-acre plot were sold in an auction. J.J.J. bought it and sold it immediately afterwards for a profit. The farmer-chief was also ruined. He had sold his grade-cows – all Friesians – in expectation of plenty as an M.P. J.J.J. saw to it that he never got back his old job of a location chief.

You go to Makueni Chang'aa Bar where Wahinya used to drink in his last days and you'll find the ruined two, now best friends, waiting for anybody who might buy them a can or two of KMK — Kill me Quick. It costs fifty only, they'll tell you.

J.J.J. still rides in a Mercedes Benz – this time 660S – just like mine – and looks at me with, well, suspicion! Four years from now . . . you never know.

Gentlemen . . . how about one for the road?

THE MUBENZI TRIBESMAN

The thing one remembers most about prison is the smell: the smell of shit and urine, the smell of human sweat and breath. So when Waruhiu shrank from contact with the passing crowd, it was not merely that he feared someone would recognize him. Who would? None of his tribesmen lived here. The crowd hurrying to the tin shacks, to the soiled fading-white chalked walls with 'Fuck you' and other slogans smeared all over, scribbled on pavements even, Christ, what a home; this crowd had never belonged to him and his kind. Waruhiu could never bear the stench of sizzling meat roasted next to overflowing bucket lavatories: he and his tribesmen always made a detour of these African locations or kept strictly to the roads. Now he recognized the stench. It reminded him of prison. Yes. There was an unmistakable suggestion of prison even in the way these locations had been cast miles away from the city centre and decent residential areas, and maintained that way by the Wabenzi tribesmen who had inherited power from their British forefathers, for fear, one imagined, and Waruhiu accepted, the stench might scare away the rare game: TOURIST. *Keep the City Clean*. But these people did not behave like prisoners. They laughed and shouted and sang and their defiant gaiety overcame the stench and the squalor. Waruhiu imagined that everyone could smell his own stench and know. There was no gaiety about his clothes or about the few tufts of hair sprouting on his big head. The memory of it made him bleed inside and again he imagined that these people could see. And he saw these voices lifted into one chorus of laughter pointing at him: they would have their revenge: one of the Wabenzi tribesmen had fallen low. The shame of it. This pained him even more than the memory of cold concrete floor for a bed, the cutting of grass with the other convicts, the white calico shorts and shirt, and the askari who all the time stood on guard. The shame would reach his friends, his wife and his children in years to come. *Your father was once in prison. Don't you play with us, son of a thief. Papa, you know what they were saying in school.* Tears. *Is it true, is it true?* And the neighbours with a shake of the head: *We do not understand. How could a man with such education, earning so much, what couldn't we do with his salary.* The shame of it.

That is what galled him most. He had been to a university college and had obtained a good degree. He was the only person from his village with such distinction. When people in the village learnt he was going to college, they all, women, men and children, flocked to his home. *You have a son.* And the happy proud faces of his parents. The wrinkles seemed to have temporarily disappeared. This hour of glory and recognition. The reward of all their labour in the settled area. *He is a son of the village. He will bring the whiteman's wisdom to our ridge.* And when the time came for him to leave, it was no longer a matter between him and his parents. People came to the party even from the surrounding villages. The songs of pride. The admiration from the girls. And the young men hid their envy and befriended him. It was also the hour of the village priest. *Take this Bible. It's your spear and shield.* The old man too. *Always remember your father and mother. We all are your parents. Never betray the people.* Altogether it had been too much for him and when he boarded the train he vowed to come back and serve the people. Vows and Promises.

The college was a new world. Small but larger. Fuller. New men. New and strange ideas. And with the other students they discussed the alluring fruits of this world. *The whiteman is going. Jobs. Jobs. Life.* He still remembered the secret vow. He would always stand or fall by his people.

In his third year he met Ruth. Or rather he fell in love. He had met her at college dances and socials. But the moment she allowed him to walk her to her hall of residence, he knew he would never be happy without her. Aah, Ruth. She could dress. And knew her colours. It was she who popularized straightened hair and wigs at college. You have landed a true Negress even without going to America, the other boys used to say. And their obvious envy increased his pride and pleasure. That's why he could not resist a college wedding. She wanted it. It was good. He was so proud of her as she leaned against him for the benefit of the cameras. Suddenly he wished his parents were present. To share this moment. Their son and Ruth.

Should he not have invited them? He asked himself afterwards. Ruth's parents had come. She had not told him. It was meant as a joke, a wedding surprise for him. Maybe it was as well. Ruth's parents were, well, rich. Doubts lingered. Perhaps he ought to have waited and married a girl who knew the village and its ways. But could he find a girl who would meet his intellectual and social requirements? He was being foolish. He loved this girl. Oh my Negress. She was an African. Suppose he had gone to England or America and married a white woman. Therein was real betrayal. All the same he felt he should have invited his parents and vowed not to be so negligent in future. In any case when they saw the bride he would bring home on top of his brilliant academic record! He felt better. He told her about the village and his secret vows. I hope you will be happy in the village. Don't be silly. Of course I shall. You know my father and mother are illiterate. Come, come. Stop fretting. As if I was not an African myself. You don't know how I hate cities. I want to be a daughter of the soil. Ruth came from one of the rich families that had early embraced Christianity and exploited the commercial possibilities of the new world. She had grown up in the city and the ways of the country were a bit strange to her. But her words reassured him. He felt better and loved her all the more.

His return to the village was a triumphal entry. People again flowed to his father's compound to see him. She looks like a whitewoman, people whispered in admiration. Look at her hair.

Her nails. Stockings. His aged father with a dirty blanket across his left shoulder, fixed his eyes on him. Father, this is my wife. His mother wept with joy. For weeks after the couple was all the talk of the area. She is so proud. Ssh. Do you not know that she too has all the wisdom of the whiteman, just like our son?

A small, three-roomed house had been built for them. He became a teacher. Ruth worked in the big city. They lived happily.

For a time.

She started to fret. Life in a mud hut without electricity, without music, was suffocating. The constant fight against dirt and mud was wearying. She resented the many villagers who daily came to the house and stayed late. She could not have the privacy she so needed, especially with her daily journeys to the city and back. And the many relatives who flocked daily with this or that problem. Money. She broke down and wept. I wish you would ask them all to go. I am so tired. Oh, Ruth, you know I can't, it's against custom. Custom! Custom! And she became restless. And because he loved her and loved the village, he was hurt, and became unhappy. Let's go and live in the town, we can get a house at the newly integrated residential area, I'll pay the rent. They went. He too was getting tired of the village and the daily demands.

She kept her money. He kept his. He gave up teaching. The amount of money he would get as a teacher even in the city would be too small to meet the new demands of an integrated neighbour-hood, as they preferred to call the area. An oil company was the answer. He worked in the Sales Department. His salary was fatter. But he soon found that a town was not a village and the new salary was not as big as he had imagined. To economize, he gradually discontinued support for his countless relatives. Even this was not enough. He had joined a new tribe and certain standards were expected of him and other members. He bought a Mercedes S220. He also bought a Mini Morris – a shopping basket for his wife. This was the fashion among those who had newly arrived and wanted to make a mark. There were the house gadgets to buy and maintain if he was to merit the respect of his new tribesmen. And of course the parties. He joined the Civil Servants Club, formerly exclusively white.

His wife spent her money mostly on food and clothes. She would not trust him with any of it because she feared he might spend it on the troublesome relatives. But he had to keep up with the others. Could he shame her in front of the other wives? The glory of their days at college came back. He was grateful and stopped even the four visits to his parents because he had no money and she would not go with him. And because his salary was now too small – house rent, a Mercedes Benz and the shopping basket, all to be paid for – he began to 'borrow' the company's money that came his way. Of course I shall return it, he told himself. Still he learnt to play with the company's cheques. When at last he was caught, the amount he had consumed was more than he could pay.

Waruhiu left one street and quickly crossed to the next. Though he hated the locations, it was easier to hide there, in the crowd until darkness came. He did not want to meet any of his tribesmen while his body exuded the stench. At night he would take a bus which would take him to the only place he would get welcome. He loved Ruth. She loved him. Her love would wash away the stench – even the shame. After all, had he not done those things for her? As for his village, he would not show his face there. How could he look all those people in the eyes? As he waited for the bus, the last scene in the courtroom came back.

The case had attracted much attention. The village priest and people from his home had come. The press with their cameras. First offender. Six months with a warning to all educated to set an example. This was a new Kenya. As he was led out of the crowded courtroom, he saw tears on his mother's face. Many of the villagers had grave, averted faces. Hand-cuffed hour of shame. He put on a brave, haughty front. But within, he wept.

His one consolation was that Ruth was not in the court. He would have died to see her pain and public shame.

The bus came. And the darkness. He looked forward to seeing Ruth. Had she changed much? She was a tall slim woman, not beautiful, but she had grace and power. He would take her in his arms, breaking her fragrant grace on his broad breast. Perhaps the stench would go. That was all he now wanted. He was sure she would understand. In bed, she had always been able to still his doubts and he always discovered faith in the power of renewed love. Ruth. He would not seek work in this city. He would go to one of the neighbouring countries. He would begin all over. He now knew wisdom. He would live faithfully by her side. He had failed the village. He had failed his mother and father. He would never fail Ruth. Never.

He came out of the bus. He knew this place. The smell of roses and bougainvillea. The fresh, crisp air. The wide spaces between houses. What a difference from the locations. Here, he was the only person with strong stench. But he already felt purified as he walked to his house and Ruth. He could not bear the mounting excitement.

Near the door, and he heard a new voice, a deep round voice. He felt utter despair. So his wife had moved! How was he to find her new house.

He gathered courage and knocked at the door. At least he would try to find out if she had left her new address. He stepped aside, into the shadows. The sound of high-heeled shoes; how that sound would have pleased him; the turning of the key; how he would have danced with joy. A woman stood there. For a moment he lost his voice. His legs were heavy. Desire suddenly seized him. Ruth, he whispered. It's me. Oh, she groaned. Ruth, he whispered again, don't be afraid, he continued emerging from the shadows, arms wide open to receive her. Don't, don't, she cried, after an awkward silence, and moved a step back. But it's me, he now pleaded. Go away, she sobbed, I don't know you, I don't. Please – he hesitated. Then came a hard gritty voice he had never heard in her: I'll call the police, if you don't clear off my premises: and she shut the door in his face.

He was numb all over. The stench from his body was too much even for his nostrils. All around him people drunkenly drove past. Music and forced laughter and high-pitched voices – laughter so familiar, reached him with a vengeance. Suddenly he started laughing, a hoarse ugly laughter. He laughed as he walked away; he laughed until his ribs pained; and the music and high-pitched voices still issued from the houses in this very cosmopolitan suburban estate, to compete with laughter that had turned to tears of self-hatred and bitterness.

Titles by Ngugi published by Heinemann

Weep Not, Child

The River Between

A Grain of Wheat

Petals of Blood

Devil on the Cross

Matigari

Detained: A Writer's Prison Diary (AWS 240)

The Trial of Dedan Kimathi (with Micere Mugo, AWS 191)

I Will Marry When I Want (with Ngugi wa Mirii, AWS 246)

The Black Hermit (AWS 51)

Secret Lives (AWS 150)